Santa, BABY

Santa, BABY

JENNIFER CRUSIE
LORI FOSTER
CARLY PHILLIPS

ST. MARTIN'S PAPERBACKS

"Christmas Bonus" previously appeared in *All I Want for Christmas* in 2000.

"Naughty Under the Mistletoe" previously appeared in *Naughty or Nice?* in 2001.

SANTA, BABY

ISBN: 0-312-93976-0
EAN: 978-0312-93976-2

Printed in the United States of America

St. Martin's Paperbacks edition / November 2006

St. Martin's Paperbacks are published by St. Martin's Press, 175 Fifth Avenue, New York, NY 10010.

10 9 8 7 6 5 4 3 2 1

Contents

✳

Santa, BABY

Hot Toy

Jennifer Crusie

For Nicky
whose glorious smile will defeat
every Evil Nemesis

Acknowledgments

Thank you to
Jennifer Enderlin,
who asked me to write a Christmas
romance novella
and then didn't blink when the guns and
the gin showed up;
Meg Ruley,
who turned the birthday paper into
Christmas paper;
the Cherries
who read the first scene and made
pointed suggestions;
and Bob Mayer,
who said, "You know, toys are
made in China . . ."

Chapter 1

Trudy Maxwell pushed her way through the crowded old toy store, fed up with Christmas shopping, Christmas carols, Christmas in general, and toy stores in particular. Especially this toy store. For the worst one in town, it had an awful lot of people in it. *Probably only on Christmas Eve,* she thought, and stopped a harried-looking teenager wearing an apron and a name tag, accidentally smacking him with her lone shopping bag as she caught his arm. "Oh. Sorry. Listen, I need a Major MacGuffin."

The kid pulled his arm away. "You and everybody else, lady."

"Just tell me where they are," Trudy said, not caring she was being dissed by somebody who probably couldn't drive yet. Anything to get a homicidal doll that spit toxic waste.

"When we had them, they were in the back, row four, to the right. But those things have been gone since before Thanksgiving." The kid shrugged. "You shoulda tried eBay."

"And I would have, if I hadn't just found out I needed it today," Trudy said with savage cheerfulness. "So, row four, to the right? Thank you."

She threaded her way through the crowd, heading for the back of the store. Above her, Madonna cooed "Santa Baby," the ancient store speakers making the carol to sex and greed sound a little tinny. Whatever had happened to "The Little Drummer Boy"? That had been annoying, too, but in a traditional way, like fruitcake. She'd be happy to hear a "rum-pa-pum-pum" again, anything that didn't make Christmas sound like it was about getting stuff.

Especially since she was desperate to get some stuff.

The crowd thinned out as she got to the back

of the store. Halfway down the last section of the fourth row, she found the dusty, splintered wood shelf marked with a card that said: *Major MacGuffin, the Tough One Two*. It was, of course, empty.

"Damn," she said, and turned to look at the shelf next to it, hoping a careless stock boy might have—

Six feet two of broad-shouldered, dark-haired grave disappointment stood there, looking as startled as she was, and her treacherous heart lurched sideways at the sight.

"Uh, merry Christmas, Trudy," Nolan Mitchell said, clearly wishing he were somewhere else.

Yes, this makes my evening, she thought, and turned away.

"Trudy?"

"I don't talk to strangers," Trudy said over her shoulder, and tried to ignore her pounding heart to concentrate on the lack of MacGuffins in front of her. She'd been polite and well behaved with Nolan Mitchell for three dates and he'd still dumped her, so the hell with him.

"Look, I'm sorry I didn't call—"

"I really don't care," Trudy said, keeping her back to him. "In October, I cared. In November, I decided you were a thoughtless, inconsiderate loser. And in December, I forgot all about you."

Madonna sang, "Been an awful good girl,"

and Trudy thought, *Like I had a choice*. The least he could have done was seduce her before he abandoned her.

"It's not like I seduced and abandoned you," he said, and when she turned and glared at him, he added, "Okay, wrong thing to say. I really am sorry I didn't call. Work got crazy—"

"You're a literature professor," Trudy said. "*Chinese* literature. How can that get craz—" She shook her head. "Never mind. You didn't like me, you didn't call, I don't care." She turned back to the shelf, concentrating on not concentrating on Nolan. So it was empty. That didn't necessarily mean there were no MacGuffins. Maybe—

"Okay, I'm the rat here," Nolan said, with the gravelly good humor in his voice that had made her weaken and agree to go out the fourth time he'd asked her even though he was a lit professor, even though she'd known better.

The silence stretched out and he added, "It was rude and inconsiderate of me."

She thought, *So he has a nice voice, so he's sorry, big deal*, and tried hard to ignore him, and then he said, "Come on. It's Christmas. Peace on earth. Goodwill to men. I'm a man."

You certainly are, her id said.

We've been through this, she told her baser self. *He's no good. We don't like him. He's bad for us.*

"Okay, so you've forgotten I exist. That means we can start over." He came around her and stuck his hand out. "Hi. I'm Nolan Mitchell and I—"

"No," Trudy said, annoyed with herself for wanting to take his hand. "We can't start over. You were a grave disappointment. Grave disappointments do not get do-overs."

She turned away again and put her mind back on the MacGuffin. Okay, this was the worst toy store in the city, so the inventory control had to be lousy. If somebody had shoved a box to one side . . .

She dropped her shopping bag and began to methodically take down the faded boxes of toys to the right of the empty MacGuffin shelf. They were ancient but evidently not valuable *Star Wars* figures, a blast from her past. There was a little Han Solo in Nolan, she thought. Maybe that was why she'd fallen for him. It wasn't him at all, it was George Lucas and that damn light saber. She put Nolan out of her mind and kept taking down boxes until she reached the last layer. None of them were MacGuffins.

"Trudy, look, I—"

"Go *away;* I have problems."

"You have *Star Wars* problems?"

"No. I have Major MacGuffin problems. If you know where to get one, I will talk to you. Otherwise, leave."

"I can't." Nolan smiled at her sheepishly. "I'm looking for a MacGuffin, too."

"I figured you more for the Barbie type." Trudy started to stack the boxes back on the shelf again.

"No, no, I'm a collector." Nolan picked up a box and put it back for her, and she thought about telling him to go away again, but she really didn't want to put all the boxes back by herself. "It's important to get the toys mint in the box." He held up a box with a crumpled corner. "See, this is no good."

"Thank you for sharing." Trudy put another box back. When he continued to help, she decided he could put them back by himself and moved to the dusty boxes to the left of the empty MacGuffin shelf. Action figures from *The Fantastic Four.* The store really did have an inventory problem; those were completely out-of-date. Well, if there wasn't a Mac to the right, there would be one to the left. Life could not be so cruel as to send her a Nolan but not a MacGuffin.

She began to methodically remove every *Fantastic Four* box on the shelf, while Nolan restocked the *Star Wars* figures and tried to make small talk about the MacGuffin, asking her if she'd bought one there before, if she shopped in the store often, if she knew anybody who'd bought one there. She ignored him until she'd pulled out the last box and there was still no MacGuffin, and then she took a deep breath. Okay, Plan B. Maybe on the other side of the shelf . . .

"Trudy, I—"

"Unless you have a MacGuffin, I'm not interested."

"Okay," he said. "I understand." He put the last of the *Star Wars* boxes back and smiled at her. "Have a great Christmas and a happy new year, Trudy."

He turned to go and she turned back to the shelf, irrationally depressed that he was going. She *wanted* him to go, that was the *point*—

She heard him say, "Hello, Reese," and then somebody else said, "Hey, I heard you guys talking about the MacGuffins. You found any?" and Trudy looked up to see the kind of guy who looked like he'd say "dude" a lot: early twenty-something, clueless face, muscled shoulders, tousled hair. The only non-surfer thing about him was his shopping bag with a pink confetti-printed box sticking out of the top. Both the box and the guy looked vaguely familiar, but Trudy couldn't place either one.

He grinned at her. "Hey, Miss Maxwell, you're lookin' good."

Trudy looked closer but still didn't recognize him.

"You don't remember me." His grin widened with forgiveness, and he added, "I sure remember you," and Trudy thought, *What a shame he's too young for me. I could seduce him in front of Nolan.*

He stepped closer. "I'm Reese Daniels, your father's research assistant last year. You helped me find that book on the Ming Dynasty your father wanted. You know, in the library."

"Good place to find books," Nolan said, his voice considerably cooler than it had been when he'd talked to her.

"Right. Reese. Got it," Trudy said, placing him now as the guy her father had called the most inept RA of his career.

Reese smiled at her. "I sure have missed your dad since he went to London."

"Oh, we all have," Trudy lied, and stuck out her hand. "Call me Trudy." She looked at Nolan. "You can call me Miss Maxwell," she said to him. "No, wait, you're not going to call me at all. Weren't you leaving?" Reese still held on to her hand, so she took it back.

He nodded to Nolan. "So you and Professor Mitchell found a MacGuffin?"

"Professor Mitchell and I are not together." Trudy picked up her shopping bag and moved around both of them. "And I haven't found a MacGuffin yet. But I will."

Reese followed her around to the next row and the other side of the empty MacGuffin shelf. "Well, I'm not sorry you're not with Professor Mitchell, Trudy," he said when they'd rounded the corner. "I never got the chance to get to know you better. Your dad worked me pretty hard. But the best part about being his RA was always seeing you."

"Thank you." Okay, for some reason this infant was trying to pick her up. Whatever. She had problems, so later for him.

Trudy zeroed in on the boxes that backed up against the MacGuffin shelf. Dolls this time, with big heads and miniskirts and too much eye makeup. Too bad Leroy wasn't a girl; she could have loaded him up with poptarts. But no, he had to have a violent, antisocial 'Guffin.

"Men." She put her shopping bag down again and began to take the dolls off the shelf. Over the tops she could see Nolan restocking *Fantastic Fours*. He shook his head at her, probably disgusted she was flirting with an infant like Reese, and she turned away to see the infant looking at her, confused.

"Men?" he said. "Did I say something wrong?"

"What?" Trudy said, stacking doll boxes on the floor. "Oh, not you. My nephew, Leroy. He's five and he wants a Major MacGuffin doll, and of course, I can't find one."

"Yeah, you had to shop early for those," Reese said, sounding sympathetic. "So I guess you haven't seen one here?"

"I would have shopped early if I'd known his father wasn't going to get him one," Trudy said, exasperated. "But since his father told me he was going to, I didn't."

"So what are you doing over here?" Reese frowned, looking at the dolls she was taking down.

"I'm looking for a misplaced MacGuffin. This place is pretty sloppy, and I'm hoping there's one stuck at the back of a shelf someplace because if there isn't, I'm screwed." She took the last box down and faced another empty shelf.

On the other side, Nolan looked serious as he put back the last of the Fantastic Four boxes. He couldn't possibly care that she was talking to Reese. Unless he was one of those guys who didn't want something until somebody else wanted it. He hadn't seemed like that kind of guy.

He'd seemed pretty much perfect: smart, funny, kind, thoughtful . . .

Ignore him, she told herself, and started to put the boxes back. *Okay, suppose I was hiding a toy so I could come back and get it later, maybe when I had more money. I found the last MacGuffin, but I didn't have enough to pay for it, so I needed to hide it. The first thing I'd do is go to another row of shelves so nobody who wanted one would trip over it accidentally.*

Nolan came around the end of the shelf and started to say something and then saw all the doll boxes on the floor. "Great."

Trudy ignored him to smile at Reese and then picked up her bag to go look in a different aisle.

"So no MacGuffin," Reese said. "Really sorry about that."

"Yep," Trudy said, and then stopped when she caught another glimpse of the pink confetti-patterned box sticking out of Reese's shopping bag. "What is that?"

He looked down. "This? It's some nail polish doll my niece wanted."

Nail polish doll? Trudy reached down and pulled the box out of the bag. "Oh, my God," she said, looking closer at the Pepto-Bismol pink box that said: *Twinkletoes!* in silver sparkly paint. "This doll is twenty-five years old!"

"I think it's a reissue," Reese said, sounding confused as he tried to take it back.

"Is the box mint?" Nolan said, and Reese frowned at him and tugged on the box again.

"A reissue." Trudy held on to the box. Her sister would have a heart attack if she knew they were making these again. She brought the box closer to see through the clear plastic. Yep, it was the same pouting blonde bimbo, Princess Twinkletoes, and there at the bottom next to Twinkletoes' fat little feet was the same pink plastic manicure set with three heart-shaped bottles of polish—pink, silver, and purple—that had made Courtney's six-year-old heart beat faster, the Hot Toy of 1981. "Where did you get this?"

Reese yanked the box from her hands and nodded to the next row. "Over there," he said, sliding the box back into his bag. "There are a lot of them."

Trudy rounded the corner to see the Twinkletoes shelf, crammed full of hot pink boxes. Evidently lightning did not strike twice; Twink was clearly not the Hot Toy of 2006. *You get a little age on you and nobody wants you,* Trudy thought. Well, unless you were Barbie. That bitch lasted forever. Trudy picked up a Twinkletoes box.

Reese came to stand beside her. "Your nephew wants a doll?"

"This is the doll my little sister never got," Trudy said. *And she could use some payback this Christmas.*

"How old's your little sister?"

"Thirty-one."

"Oh."

Trudy looked up at the confusion in his voice. "Courtney was supposed to get this the Christmas she was six, but my dad forgot. He told her it fell off Santa's sleigh."

"Uh huh," Reese said, probably trying to picture her academic father talking about Santa.

"That was his line for whenever he forgot the Christmas presents," Trudy said, thinking of Leroy, waiting at home for his MacGuffin. If she didn't find a MacGuffin, would she be reduced to the "fell off the sleigh" line?

Never.

"Did he forget a lot?" Reese said, sympathy in his voice.

"Pretty much every year. You know professors. Absentminded." Trudy shook her head. "Never mind. I'm rambling. My mind's on my sister and my nephew."

"Well, hey, it's Christmas. That's where your mind is supposed to be. Family." Reese smiled at her, gripping his own Twinkletoes box. "Listen, I have to get going, but maybe we can have coffee sometime?"

"Sure." Trudy smiled back at him automatically, her mind on the Twinkletoes. Would a gift that was a couple of decades late distract Courtney from her divorce?

Hell, it couldn't hurt.

Reese walked away, and she looked closer at the Twinkletoes box in her hands. It had a crumpled corner and she remembered what Nolan had said. The box should be mint. She put her shopping bag down and began to take the Twinkletoes boxes off the shelf. Courtney was going to get a perfect Twinkletoes, pink box and all.

Nolan came around the end of the row and sighed when he saw the boxes on the floor.

"Go away." Trudy took down the next pink box.

"Listen, is there anything I can do to make you not so mad?"

"Mad? I'm not mad." Trudy studied the Twinkletoes box. Smudge on the top. She dropped it on Nolan's foot. "Why would I be mad?"

He picked it up. "That's what I asked."

She pulled another Twinkletoes box off the shelf and shoved it at him. "Okay, here's why I'm mad. I didn't want to go out with you because you were a professor, and I grew up with a professor, and it was no fun because you get forgotten a lot because your dad is thinking about something that happened four millennia ago, so I said no, four times I said no, but you kept at me and I weakened and went out and *I really liked you, you bastard,* and you were smart and you were funny"—she shoved another box at him—"and I thought, gee, maybe this will work out, maybe this is a professor who won't forget, but evidently it was just the thrill of the chase or something because you dropped me"—she threw the next box at him and he caught it, balancing it with the first two—"and I never knew why since you never bothered to tell me; you just fell right off the sleigh—"

"Sleigh?" Nolan said.

"... so *I'm a little upset with you.*"

Nolan sighed. "Look, you changed."

"Of course I changed," Trudy snapped. "It's been three months. I've grown. I've matured. I'm in a new and better place now. A place without you. Go away." She went back to the Twinkletoes shelf, pulling boxes off at random and dropping them on the floor, appalled to realize that she was close to tears. He did not matter to her; the fact that she'd thought he was darling was immaterial; the fact that she'd told her sister he might be The One was immaterial; the fact that her father had said, *Nolan Mitchell, that's a little out of your league, isn't it?* was ... Well, her father was a jerk, so that didn't count.

"No, you changed from the library," Nolan

was saying. "You were funny in the library. You talked fast and made weird jokes and surprised me. I liked that. And then I took you out and you, well, you kind of went dull on me."

Trudy stopped dropping boxes on the floor. "You took me to a faculty party. If I hadn't gone dull on you, you'd have lost points. You'd have been Nolan who brought that weird-ass librarian to the October gin fling. I was *helping you.*"

"Did I ask for help?" Nolan said, exasperated.

"And you took me to dinner at the department head's house. You wanted me weird there?"

"I couldn't get out of that," Nolan said.

"And then the Chinese film festival." Trudy dropped another box to the floor. "I thought I was going to see *Crouching Tiger Two,* but it was some horrible depressing thing about people weeping in dark rooms."

"It was?" Nolan said, confused.

"Not that you'd know, since you *left right after it started,*" Trudy snarled, flinging a box at him. "You got a call and walked out of the theater and I was left with people weeping in Chinese—"

She stopped to stare at the shelf, the next box in her hand, her heart thudding harder than it had when she'd first seen Nolan.

There was a camouflage-colored box at the back.

She dropped the Twinkletoes box and pulled out the camo box and read the label: *Major MacGuffin, the Tough One*! "Oh, my God." Trudy held on to it with both hands, almost shaking.

The box was not mint—the cellophane was torn over the opening, a corner was squashed in with a black X marked on it, and there were white scuff marks on the bottom—but the MacGuffin scowled out at her through the plastic, looking like a homicidal Cabbage Patch doll dressed in camouflage, a grenade in one hand and a gun in the other, violent and disgusting and the only thing Leroy wanted for Christmas.

"I do believe in Santa," Trudy said as Nolan came closer.

"That's a Major MacGuffin." He sounded stunned.

"Can you believe it?" Trudy was so amazed she forgot to be mad.

"No," Nolan said. "I can't. I knew you were an amazing woman, but this puts you in a whole new league."

"What?" Trudy said.

"I'll give you two hundred bucks for it," Nolan said.

"*No.*" Trudy stepped away from him, holding on to the MacGuffin box.

Nolan smiled at her, radiating sincerity. "I know, your nephew wants a Major MacGuffin, but he doesn't want that one. He wants the Mac Two. The one that spits toxic waste and packs a tac nuke, right?"

Trudy thought of Leroy, waxing rhapsodic about how the 'Guffin spit green stuff when you squeezed him. "Yes."

"What you have there is a MacGuffin One," Nolan said, sounding sympathetic and entirely too reasonable. "Last year's model. No toxic waste."

Trudy looked back at the box. It did look different from the picture Leroy had shown her. "What does this one do?"

"It has a gun. Basically, it shoots the other dolls."

"And the hand grenade?"

"Just a plastic ball. Doesn't do anything." He shrugged, unimpressed.

"Damn." Trudy looked down at the doll's ugly face.

"Two fifty," Nolan said.

Trudy glared at him. "No. This is for my nephew. And I have to go now. Thanks for putting the boxes back."

"Trudy, *wait*," Nolan said, but she picked up a perfect Twinkletoes box, stepped over the rest of the pink boxes, and headed for the checkout counter, her belief in Santa restored if not her belief in the rest of male humanity.

Trudy got in the long line to the register, clutching both the Mac and the Twinkletoes boxes, stepping back as a woman in a red and green bobble hat slid in front of her at the last minute. Then Nolan got in line behind her and said, "Three hundred. It only costs forty-nine fifty new. That's six times—"

Trudy jerked her head up. "*No.* I'll never find another one of these tonight."

Nolan nodded, not arguing. "Okay. Five hundred."

"Are you nuts?" Trudy said.

"No, I told you, I'm a collector." He stepped closer, and she remembered how nice it had been having him step closer on the three lousy dates they'd had.

She stepped away.

Nolan nodded to the Mac. "You are holding a doll that is actually rarer than the Mac Two. They didn't make many Ones."

"It's not rarer from where I'm standing," Trudy said. "I actually *have* this one, and there are no Mac Twos in sight."

"That looks like an original box," Nolan said. "May I?"

"No," Trudy said, holding on to it and the Twinkletoes box, trying to put her shopping bag between them to block him, but he'd already opened the top and was reaching in. "Hey." She elbowed his hand away as he pulled out the instruction sheet. *"Give me that,"* she said, and he opened it so that she could see the drawing of the MacGuffin showing how to detach the silencer from the gun.

"No toxic waste," Nolan said. "It's a Mac One."

He slid the instructions back in the box. "Two thousand," he said, and then Trudy heard somebody say, "I'll be damned," and turned to see Reese staring at her from the front of the checkout line.

"You found it," he said.

"Yes." She turned back to Nolan as he closed the box again. "No. I'm not selling it. This one is Leroy's." She checked to make sure the MacGuffin was still in the box, complete with hand grenade and gun, and then her cell phone rang.

She fumbled the boxes until she could hold both of them with one arm, looked at the caller ID, clicked the phone on, and said, "Hello, Courtney."

"Did you get it?" Courtney said, and Trudy pictured her, sitting on the edge of her Pottery Barn couch, her thin fingers gripping her

Restoration Hardware forties black dial phone, every auburn Pre-Raphaelite ringlet on her head wired with tension.

"Sort of." Trudy looked through the plastic window on the front of the Mac box at the fat little homicidal doll. "Damn, he's ugly."

"What do you mean, *sort of*? Did you *get him*?"

The line moved and Trudy stepped forward, bumping her shopping bag into the woman in the bobble hat.

"I'm so sorry," she said as the woman turned. "Really sorry."

The woman smiled at her, motherly in a knitted cap with red and green bobbles, her arms full of teddy bears. "Isn't it just awful, this Christmas rush? . . ."

Her eyes narrowed as she saw the MacGuffin. Animals in the bush probably looked like that when they sighted their prey. Trudy clutched the MacGuffin box tighter.

The woman jerked her face up to Trudy's. "Where did you get that?"

"In the back, shoved behind some other boxes." Trudy tried to sound cheerful and open. "Boy, did I get lucky."

The woman's chin went up. "That's not this year's."

"No toxic waste." Trudy nodded. "Well, you can't have everything."

"I'll give you a hundred dollars for it," the woman said, her eyes avid.

Piker. "No, thank you."

"Who are you talking to?" Courtney said, her voice crackling with phone static.

"A lovely woman who just tried to buy the MacGuffin from me."

"No!"

"Of course not, but listen, I've got last year's model. The Mac One. I don't think—"

"Evil Nemesis Brandon is getting this year's model. The Mac Two. With extra toxic waste."

Trudy shifted her weight to her other foot. "Okay, this 'Evil Nemesis Brandon' stuff? You have to stop that. Do you want Leroy thrown out of kindergarten for calling names?"

"Evil Nemesis Brandon's mother knows we don't have a Mac," Courtney said. "I saw her today at Stanford Trudeau's Christmas party. She said if we hadn't found one, Brandon would let Leroy borrow his last year's doll."

"Okay, she's a terrible person, but you have to stop calling her kid names."

Trudy shifted the boxes, trying not to drop either one, and the eyes of the woman in front of her followed the Mac box. A man with a cap with earflaps, standing in front of the woman in front of Trudy, looked back idly and then froze and said, "Is that a Major MacGuffin?"

"Last year's model," Trudy said to him, and shifted the boxes again. *It's like being on the veldt. Gazelle vs. lions.*

The woman in front of her stepped closer, and Trudy backed up and bumped into Nolan.

Lots of lions.

"Do you have any idea *how humiliating that was*?" Courtney was saying. "Do you have any idea—"

"Well, that's what you get for going to a cocktail party while I'm busting my butt searching for a nonexistent war toy." The line moved up and Trudy followed, praying she wouldn't drop the Mac box. There'd be a bloodbath if she did. "I'm all for you getting out and playing well with others, but it's Christmas Eve and you should be home with your family, baking something, not looking for your second husband. I'm sure Stanford Trudeau is a lovely man with an excellent retirement portfolio, but—"

"I'm baking gingerbread men *and* a gingerbread house right now, and Stanford Trudeau is five. It was Leroy's playgroup's Christmas party. And that woman *mocked* me."

Trudy took a deep breath and reminded herself that Courtney had troubles. "Okay, so now you can tell her he has his own last year's doll. I'm getting ready to buy it right now."

"Last year's is not good enough!" Courtney said, her voice rising.

"Oh, get a grip. This one is a collector's item. It has a hand grenade."

"And a gun," Nolan said from too close behind her, obviously listening in.

"And a gun," Trudy told Courtney as she ignored Nolan.

"Who said that?" Courtney said. "Who's with you?"

"Nolan."

"Nolan." Courtney sounded confused and then she said, *"Nolan Mitchell.* The Chinese lit prof with the swivel hips you thought was going to be The One?"

"Yes," Trudy said, cursing her sister's excellent memory.

"Whoa," Courtney said. "He's the only guy you ever wore sensible shoes for."

"I just ran into him," Trudy said repressively. "It was an accident. It will not happen again."

"It could happen again," Nolan said.

"I don't believe in The One anymore," Trudy told Courtney, ignoring him. "But he is right that this Mac has a gun. Very convenient. It can shoot the other dolls."

"That's not funny."

"Well, I don't think so, either." Trudy shifted the boxes again, making the woman in front of her twitch. "This is a really horrible toy, Court."

"I mean it's not funny that it's not this year's. Leroy has been talking about toxic waste for weeks."

"See, that's not a good thing."

"Two hundred," the woman in front of her said.

"No." Trudy shifted the box again. "Listen—"

"Leroy says that Evil Nemesis Brandon—"

"Will you stop calling him that? I don't believe for one moment that Leroy came up with 'Evil Nemesis Brandon' on his own. That was you."

"That was Prescott," Courtney said, loathing in her voice for her AWOL husband. "But Leroy cares. A lot. He . . . Wait a minute. Talk to him."

"Court, no—"

Trudy heard the phone clunk as the line moved up a couple of feet. She stepped forward, thinking, *At least Courtney will have the Twinkletoes this year*. Courtney had been waiting to polish those toes for twenty-five years.

And now poor little Leroy would probably be waiting another twenty-five years for his toxic waste. She had a vision of herself many years in the future, handing the Mac Two to a sad-eyed thirty-year-old hopeless wreck of a nephew.

"Three hundred," the woman in the cap said.

"*No.*" Trudy heard the phone clank again and then she heard her nephew's voice, bright as ever.

"Aunt Trudy?"

"Hey, bad, bad Leroy," she said, smiling as she pictured his happy little face under his shock of little-boy-blond hair. "Isn't it time you were in bed?"

"Yes. And then Santa will bring me a 'Guffin. Hurry up and come home so you can see."

"You know, Leroy," Trudy said, looking at the box in her arms. "There are several kinds of MacGuffins and they're all good—"

"I want the one with toxic waste," Leroy said clearly. "It's okay. I told Daddy, and he told Santa, and Santa said he'd bring one. And Nanny Babs said Santa never lies."

I'm going to kill that fucking son of a bitch. And then I'm going to kill that fucking nanny. Assuming they ever come back from Cancún. "Well, we'll just have to see, won't we? Now you go to bed—"

"I know, and when I wake up, Daddy will be on vacation, but he loves me, and Santa will be here with my 'Guffin." He breathed heavily into the phone for a moment and then said, "Brandon said there isn't any Santa Claus."

Rot in hell, Evil Nemesis Brandon. "What do you think?"

"I think there is," Leroy said, not sounding too sure. "And I think he's going to bring me a 'Guffin tomorrow."

"Right," Trudy said, holding on to the box tighter.

"With toxic waste," Leroy said.

Oh, just hell. "Merry Christmas Eve, baby. Go to bed."

"Aunt Trudy?"

"Five hundred," the woman in front of her said. "And that's my final offer."

"For the love of God, *no*," Trudy said to her, and then said, "Yes, Leroy?"

"Do you believe in Santa?"

What is this, a movie of the week? "Well . . ."

"Mommy says Evil Nemesis Brandon is wrong."

"Don't call him that, sweetie."

"Is he wrong?" Leroy's voice slowed. "It's okay if there isn't a Santa." His voice said it wasn't okay.

Nolan nudged her gently and she realized the line had moved again. "Well, Leroy, I don't really know if there's a Santa. I've never seen him."

"Oh."

Trudy swallowed. "But that doesn't mean there isn't one. I've never seen SpongeBob, either."

"SpongeBob?" Nolan said from behind her.

"SpongeBob is real. He's on TV." Leroy sounded relieved. "So is Santa."

"Well, there you go," Trudy said, feeling like a rat.

"That's the best you've got, SpongeBob?" Nolan said.

Trudy turned and snarled, "He loves SpongeBob. Shut up."

"I know there's a SpongeBob," Leroy said, happy again.

"As do we all," Trudy said.

The woman in front of her let her breath out between her teeth, clearly frustrated. "It's the old MacGuffin; it's not worth more than three hundred."

"I'm sure you're right," Trudy said to her. "Leroy? Honey, it's time for you to go to bed."

"And when I wake up, I'll get a 'Guffin," Leroy said. "Good night, Aunt Trudy."

"Good night, baby," Trudy said, and the phone clunked again as he dropped it.

"Your nephew's name is Leroy?" Nolan said.

"It's a nickname," Trudy said, not turning around. "His real name is Prescott Thurston Brown II."

"Oh." He paused. "Good call getting a nickname."

She heard the phone clunk again as Courtney picked it up.

"That little bastard Brandon," Courtney said.

"I think I prefer 'Evil Nemesis,'" Trudy said. "He's just a kid, Courtney."

"His mother is a hag," Courtney said. "After she offered Leroy a hand-me-down MacGuffin, she asked me if I'd found another nanny."

"Bitch," Trudy said, and then smiled when the woman in front of her finally turned away, offended.

"He's counting on that toxic waste." Courtney's voice was still teary, but now she sounded a little slack.

"Court? You haven't been hitting the eggnog, have you?"

"No, the gin. I'm a terrible mother, Tru."

"No, you're not." Trudy shifted the boxes again.

"I can't even get my baby toxic waste for Christmas."

Trudy heard her sob. "Okay, step away from the gin. You're getting sloppy drunk in front of your kid. Do something proactive. Wrap some presents. Ice your gingerbread."

"I'm out of Christmas paper. And I tried to ice those little bastard gingerbread men, but their arms kept breaking off."

"Were you twisting them?"

Above Trudy's head, the ancient speakers blared Madonna singing in baby talk again.

"Sing 'The Little Drummer Boy,'" Trudy said to the speakers. "Anything but 'Santa Baby.' God, Madonna is annoying."

"She's a good mother," Courtney said. "I'm a *terrible mother*."

"No, you just have terrible taste in husbands and nannies."

"I wasn't the one who picked out the nanny," Courtney said, her voice rising.

"Right." Trudy moved up another step. "Sorry. She came highly recommended." *I'm pretty sure yours is the first husband she ran off with.*

"I wasn't the one who brought home the husband, either," Courtney cried.

"Okay," Trudy said, tempted to fight back on that one.

"I'm being punished, aren't I?" Courtney said. "I stole my sister's boyfriend—"

"Ten years ago," Trudy said. "I'm over it. I was over it before you stole him. You're not being punished. I didn't want him, which I told you at the time. He's a jerk, I have an affinity for jerks—"

"Hey," Nolan said.

"—and you're better off without him."

"But not without the MacGuffin!"

"I'm *working on that*." Trudy looked around the last toy store in town. *How the hell am I going to get this year's MacGuffin?* "I'll get it, Court."

"And two toxic wastes," Courtney said, gulping.

"Two toxic wastes. Got it." Maybe if she just stuck the toxic-waste packets in the MacGuffin box, Leroy wouldn't notice the doll didn't actually spit it.

"And wrapping paper," Courtney said, sounding less frantic.

"Right." Trudy grabbed a package of red-and-white paper off the rack that came before the checkout counter and snagged a roll of Scotch tape while she was at it. "Got it. I gotta go. Go do something besides drink."

"*This year's* MacGuffin," Courtney said.

"Your gingerbread is burning," Trudy said, and clicked off the phone.

"Trouble at home?" Nolan said, sounding sympathetic.

"Absolutely not. Everything is *fine*."

He reached past her, nudging her gently with his shoulder as he pulled two bright green foil packages off the counter rack. "You'll need these."

He dropped them on top of the MacGuffin box and she saw the words *Toxic Waste!* emblazoned on them in neon red.

"Thank you," she said, and then the woman in the bobble cap picked up her bags and left and Trudy dumped everything onto the counter.

The cashier looked at the MacGuffin box with something approaching awe. "Where'd you find this?"

"On a shelf behind some other boxes," Trudy said for what she sincerely hoped was the last time.

"Man, did you ever get lucky," the cashier said, and began to ring it up.

"That's me," Trudy said, trying to forget that Nolan was about to leave her again, that the wrong MacGuffin was in front of her, and that Madonna was still lisping about greed overhead. "Nothing but luck, twenty-four-seven."

"A thousand," Nolan said from behind her when she'd handed over her credit card and seen the MacGuffin go in one shopping bag and the Twinkletoes in another. "Come on; that's a damn good offer."

"No," Trudy said, picked up her bags, and left.

Fifteen minutes later, Trudy stood on the street corner, juggling her three shopping bags and signaling awkwardly for a cab. There was one around the corner that was stubbornly off duty, and every other one that went by had people in the backseat. They were probably just circling the block to annoy her. She shifted the bags again, her feet aching as the cold from the concrete permeated the thin soles of her boots, trying to think of a way to get a Mac Two short of breaking into Evil Nemesis Brandon's house and stealing his.

It started to snow.

If I had some matches, I could strike them all and bask in the glow, Trudy thought, and then a cab pulled up in front of her and Reese opened the door.

"I got a lead on this year's MacGuffins," he said as he got out to stand in front of her. "Get in and we'll go get them."

Trudy gaped at him. "You're kidding."

"No. I know this guy."

Trudy frowned at him in disbelief. "You know this guy. I've been to every toy store in town, but you know this guy."

"Not a toy store. A warehouse."

"A warehouse. No, thank you." Trudy reached around him to signal for another cab, which passed her by, its tires crunching in the snow. She craned her neck to see around the corner, but the cab that had been there was gone. The streets were emptying out, stores starting to close. *I am so screwed,* she thought.

"Oh, come on." Reese held the cab door open for her and gestured her in. "This guy called around and found out about this warehouse where they got a shipment in, but the delivery people didn't come back for them. He says there are dozens of them there." Reese smiled at her, surfer cute. "So the warehouse guys are selling them out the back door. We're gonna pay through the nose, but hey, they've got Mac Twos."

Trudy put her hand down and tried to be practical—getting in a cab and going to a warehouse with a virtual stranger would be stupid even if he had been her father's research assistant—but the snow was falling faster, and the bags weren't getting any lighter, and the stores were closing, and Leroy still didn't have a MacGuffin. "My feet hurt."

Reese gestured to the cab again. "Sit."

Trudy sat down sideways on the backseat with her feet on the curb, balancing her three bags on her lap. "A warehouse."

"With a big shipment of Mac Twos." Reese looked down at her, his patience obviously wearing thin. "And I'm betting we're not the only ones who know about it, so we should get a move on."

Trudy put her forehead on her bags. The cab radio was playing some cheerful rap lite that Trudy liked until she heard the singer say, "Santa Baby."

Reese stepped closer, looming over her. "Scoot over so I can get in."

Trudy lifted her head. "For all I know you're a rapist and a murderer."

"Hey." Reese sounded wounded although he looked as clueless as ever.

"It's nothing personal. Ted Bundy was a very attractive man."

"Oh, *come on*. I worked for your dad. You're in a *cab*. You can tell the driver to wait while we go inside."

A Mac Two. It was too good to be true. Much like Reese the surfer boy hitting on an older college librarian was too good to be true. And he had a cab, too. It strained belief, something she was pretty weak in to begin with. "How did you get a cab?"

"I held out my hand and it pulled up." Reese sounded exasperated. "Look, if you don't want to go, I do. In or out."

"Oh, just hell," Trudy said.

Reese shook his head and went around to the street side of the cab and got in. "Make up your mind, Trudy," he said from behind her as he closed his door. "It's Christmas Eve and it's getting later every minute."

Okay, he'd worked with her dad, and Nolan seemed to know him from the department, and he was probably not a psychotic killer, and he said he knew where there were Mac Twos. Did she really have a choice?

She put one foot into the cab, dragging her

packages with her, keeping the other foot on the curb.

"So this warehouse," she began, and then stopped, getting a good look at the inside of the cab. It was festooned with LED Christmas lights blinking red and green in time to the music, the song's refrain whispering, "Gimme, gimme, gimme, Santa Baby." She saw Reese look up at the ceiling and followed his eyes to a shriveled piece of mistletoe safety-pinned to the sagging fabric. "My God."

"Mistletoe," Reese said.

"Pretty limp," Trudy said, squinting at it.

"I'm not."

"I have Mace."

He ducked his head and kissed her, bumping her nose, and it was nice, being kissed in a warm cab by a younger man, even if there was snow drifting in through the open door and the foot she still had on the curb was freezing. *Gimme, gimme, gimme,* Trudy thought, and wished he were Nolan.

Reese pulled back a little. "Thank you for not Macing me."

"I was thinking about it," Trudy said, and he kissed her again, putting his arms around her and pulling her close, and this time she kissed him back, because it was Christmas Eve and he might be getting her a Mac II. And because he was a pretty good kisser even if he wasn't Nolan, who was a grave disappointment anyway.

Then Nolan leaned into the cab and scared the hell out of her.

"So, where are we going?" he asked cheerfully.

"Where did you come from?" she said, her heart hammering.

"Looking for a cab." Nolan smiled at her. "Can't find one." He nudged the leg she had stretched out to the curb. "Can I share yours?"

"No," Reese said, evidently not planning on taking any classes from Nolan in the future.

"It's polite to share a cab on Christmas Eve, Mr. Daniels," Nolan said.

"I'm not polite, Professor Mitchell." Reese tightened his grip on her.

Trudy looked from one to the other. They were glaring at each other, which was sort of flattering until she remembered that they probably both wanted the Mac Two more than they wanted her. Well, there had to be safety in numbers. What were the chances they were both serial killers?

"I'm polite." Trudy pulled her foot into the cab and scooted over, stopping when her hip touched Reese's.

Nolan slid in until his hip touched hers, and shut the door.

The cab grew warmer.

"Where are we going?" he said. "Tell me it's a place with MacGuffins."

Trudy nodded. "A warehouse. With MacGuffins mint in their boxes."

"Way to go, dude," Nolan said to Reese.

"Out," Reese said, still hanging on to Trudy.

"Oh no." Trudy pulled away, leaning into Nolan in the process. "I'm only going if he goes."

"I'm touched," Nolan said.

"No, you're not," Trudy said, moving back from him again. "Safety in numbers. Any number. Not you specifically." She smiled at Reese. "We'll all go together."

Reese looked as though he might argue and then sighed. "Go," he said to the cabbie, and gave an address that Trudy knew was in the warehouse district, probably now dark and deserted and half an hour away.

Well, at least she knew Nolan wouldn't attack her. The dumbass had no interest in her body at all.

"Gimme, gimme, gimme," the radio sang.

"I hate Christmas," Trudy said, and settled back as the cab jerked into motion.

Chapter 2

So," Nolan said as the cab moved through the falling snow and the brightly lit streets. "This is really nice."

"No, it isn't," Reese said.

Actually, it was. Nolan was pressed warm against her and if she forgot everything that had happened and repressed all her common sense, it was almost like they were together again, and that felt good. *Pathetic,* she thought, but she didn't move away from him.

"What's in the other bag?" Nolan said, looking into her first shopping bag. "Is that a cow?"

"Yes," Trudy said. "It says, 'Eat chicken,' when you pull its string." He looked at her in disbelief, and she said, "Well, earlier in the evening that was hysterically funny."

"It *is* funny," Reese said, tightening his arm around her. "It's very funny."

Nolan frowned. "I hadn't figured you for the stuffed-animal-giving type," he said, taking the lanky spotted cow out of the bag.

"Really," Trudy said coolly. *I hadn't figured you for the grave-disappointment type.*

"More the educational-toy-giving type. You seem so . . . practical."

It was embarrassing to think what she had figured him for. *He's smart, he's funny, and he's got swivel hips,* she'd told Courtney. *Just imagine.* Yeah, that was the kind of statement that came back to haunt you.

"You know. You seem pretty . . . straight," Nolan said. "Being a librarian and all."

"I'm the assistant director of library sciences," she told him, trying to crush him with disdain.

"Right." Nolan nodded. "A librarian."

"Yes," Trudy said, giving up. "I'm a librarian."

Reese tightened his arm around her. "I never thought of you as a librarian. I think that's a terrible thing to call you."

Well, yeah, except I am *a librarian,* Trudy thought, and then her cell phone rang and she answered it.

"Three toxic wastes," Courtney said, her voice much looser now. "I want to bury Evil Nemesis Brandon in the stuff."

"There's no need to be unpleasant," Nolan said to Reese over her head. "It's Christmas Eve. Goodwill to men."

"Not to you," Reese said.

"Here's the situation," Trudy said to Courtney, putting one hand over her ear to shut out the cab radio—*gimme gimme gimme*—and the two guys bickering over her head. "I met one of Dad's old research assistants in the toy store and he says he knows where they have this year's MacGuffin, but it's out in some dangerous deserted warehouse on the edge of town."

"He can get one of this year's? *Yes*. Go!"

"Good to know you'll sacrifice me for a homicidal toy," Trudy said. "But that's okay; I'm already on my way."

"What's this guy's name?"

"Reese Daniels."

"Did you check his ID?"

"No, Courtney, I did not check his ID."

"Always a good idea," Nolan said. "You never know with research assistants. They can turn on you like that."

"Who's that?" Courtney said.

"Nolan."

"Still?"

"Yes," Trudy said repressively.

Reese took his wallet from his jacket, flipped it open, and showed her his driver's license.

Trudy squinted at it. "His driver's license says 'Reese Lee Daniels.' Born 1982."

"A younger man," Courtney said, distracted. "Is he cute?"

"Sort of," Trudy said. *If you like surfers. Dude.*

"I really think you and I should go out again," Nolan said. "Let's give us another chance."

Trudy closed her eyes in the dark and thought, *No, it will not work out, he'll just forget you again.*

"Do you mind?" Reese said. "She's with me."

"Forget cute," Courtney was saying on the phone. "Does he have a job? Does he look like he'll be faithful?"

"No," Trudy said to Nolan. "No more faculty, no more film."

"Okay, we'll go to the Aquarium." Nolan put

the cow back in the bag. "It'll make you calm. You can taunt the sharks."

"I bet he won't be faithful," Courtney said.

"What kind of person taunts sharks?" Trudy said to Nolan. "They're trapped in a tank."

"Okay," Nolan said, the voice of reason. "Where do you want to go? Your choice."

"Do you *mind*?" Reese said to him again. "This is my cab. Stop putting on the moves."

"I'm not asking you," Nolan said to him.

"He'll betray you," Courtney was saying gloomily. "Younger, older, they're all rats."

Trudy ignored the two guys to answer her. "That's the gin talking, honey. I thought you were going to ice gingerbread."

"I swear," Nolan said to Trudy. "No more film festivals."

Trudy waved her hand at him to get him to shut up so she could hear Courtney.

"I *am* icing gingerbread." Courtney sounded more depressed than ever. "But I broke more arms off. So I switched to the gingerbread house, and I got it together, but now the gumdrops won't stick." She sounded ready to weep.

"Why don't you wait until I get home and I can help you," Trudy said, trying to make her voice cheerful. "You probably just need thicker icing."

"Damn."

"What?"

"A gumdrop fell into my drink. Wait a minute."

Trudy listened for a moment.

"You know, they're not half bad in gin."

"Court, put the gin away and go lie down. I'll be home as soon as we get done at this warehouse, and then we'll finish the gingerbread house together."

"No more faculty parties, either," Nolan said.

Reese leaned forward, smushing Trudy between them. "She doesn't want to go out with you, *okay*?"

"That warehouse sounds dangerous," Courtney said. "Get the cab number and the cabbie's name."

Nolan shook his head at Reese. "We don't know that she doesn't want to go out with me. She never really got to know me."

"And whose fault is that?" Trudy said, turning on him. "Three dates and then you don't call, you don't write. But hey, it's not the end of the world." *And you never kissed me, either. Han Solo would have kissed me.*

"Trudy?" Courtney said.

"In a minute," Trudy said to her.

"I know, I know, that was bad of me; I'm really sorry," Nolan was saying. "But you didn't seem like you were having a good time."

"A good time? I was on my best behavior, you jerk. What else did you need? Cries of delight at the faculty party? Moans of appreciation for the movie popcorn? Which, I might point out, I ate alone. Did you think—" She stopped, realizing that arguing made it sound like she cared. "Never mind. I'm sure you had a good reason for disappearing out of my life without a reason. Forget it."

"Forget what?" Courtney said. "The name of the cabbie? You never gave it to me."

Trudy leaned over to look at the cab license for her, and Reese tightened his arm across her shoulders. "Alexander Kuroff," she said into the phone as she straightened.

"Write it down," Courtney said.

"I don't have any paper," Trudy said, and Nolan rummaged in her shopping bags and pulled out the Christmas paper she'd bought.

Trudy tore the cellophane off the corner of it and said, "No pen."

Both men offered her pens, Reese a beat behind Nolan. Trudy took Reese's and wrote the cabbie's name on the white space around the red printed words on the paper.

"And the cab number."

"Court—"

"Read it to me so I can write it down, too."

Trudy read it off. "I don't see what good my writing it down is going to do. If I die, the wrapping paper goes with me."

"You're not going to die," Nolan said. "I'm here."

"Oh, give it a rest," Reese said.

"What cab company?" Courtney said.

"Yellow Checker," Trudy said. "And I'm stopping this conversation now."

"Call me every hour," Courtney said. "If you don't call me, I'll call you. Every hour until you come home with the MacGuffin."

"What are you going to do if I don't call and I don't answer?"

"Call nine-one-one. But you're going, right?"

"I'm on my way," Trudy said, sitting back.

"Every hour," Courtney said.

"Every hour."

"I'll watch out for her," Nolan said, close to the phone.

"Who's that?" Courtney said on the phone.

"Nolan again," Trudy said. "He wants a MacGuffin, too."

"Well, at least he's the devil we know."

"We don't know him that well."

"Hey," Nolan said. "Your dad can vouch for me. We've been in the same department for two years."

"That is not a recommendation."

"What?" Courtney said.

"Dad can vouch for him."

"Push him out of the cab."

"Her dad can vouch for me, too," Reese said, sounding about twelve.

"I have to go, Court," Trudy said, before they started punching each other on the arm. "It's going to be a while." She handed Reese his pen back and started to put the wrapping paper back in the bag one-handed and then looked at it more closely in the lights from the street. "Oh, *hell*."

"What?" Courtney said.

"I got *birthday paper*," Trudy said. "I need Christmas paper, and this is *birthday*—"

"*Trudy*," Courtney wailed.

"Maybe you can fake it," Reese said, with badly concealed exasperation. "If it's just a bunch of animals, it could be anything."

Trudy held up the paper. It said *Happy Birthday* over and over and over. "No animals. Just 'Happy Birthday' in red."

"Well, then you're screwed," Reese said, sounding bored with the whole thing.

"No, she's not." Nolan held out his hand. "Give it here."

"You're going to fix this?" Trudy said. "How are you going to fix this?"

Nolan wiggled his fingers. "Gimme."

She handed the paper over and watched while he took out his pen again and wrote *Jesus* under every *Happy Birthday*.

"You're a grave disappointment, but you're also a genius," Trudy said, giving credit where it was due.

"Did he fix it?" Courtney said.

"Yes," Trudy told her.

"Make him help you get the Mac."

"*Goodbye,* Courtney," Trudy said, and hung up.

"So you'll go out with me again?" Nolan said, handing the paper back.

"Not a chance in hell." Trudy put the paper in the bag with the cow.

"Okay, lunch," Nolan said. "Lunch isn't really a date."

"Oh, give it up," Reese said, and let his head fall back against the top of the seat. "I have lost my patience with you."

"Well, look for it," Nolan said. "Maybe it fell off the sleigh."

"Man, I don't know about you," Reese said.

"I'm a man of mystery," Nolan agreed. "Another reason Trudy should see me again." He smiled at her in the dim light as the cab sped toward the warehouses. "So, meet me for coffee?"

"She doesn't want to meet you for anything," Reese said.

Yes, I do, Trudy thought.

"So, coffee," Nolan said, warm and solid beside her.

"Gimme, gimme, gimme," the voice on the radio said.

Kill me now, Trudy thought, and put her head on her shopping bags.

The streets grew dark as the cab left the city proper and turned into the warehouse district, and ten minutes later they stopped outside a deserted building, the parking lot lit by one lamp, high over its main door.

Reese opened the door and got out, holding the door for Trudy, who slid over on the seat and peered out at the darkness.

"There aren't a lot of people here buying MacGuffins," she said, staring at the empty lot.

"They probably sold out of them while you were trying to decide if I was a rapist," Reese said, sounding peeved.

"We could turn around and go back," Nolan said. "I'll buy the coffee."

Trudy took a deep breath and got out, her three shopping bags bumping against her knees.

"Want me to take those for you?" Reese said.

"No," Trudy said as Nolan got out behind her.

"You are not a trusting woman," Reese said.

"I don't think they make those anymore," Nolan said to him. "Tell you what, since you found the warehouse, I'll pay for the cab."

"Keep the cab," Trudy said, and turned back to Reese.

"The Macs are in here," Reese said, and opened the door to the warehouse.

There was light inside, but Trudy stopped at the door to wait for Nolan. He talked to the cabbie, and then he turned and came toward her and the cab drove away.

"Hey, I told you to keep the cab," she said, and Nolan took her arm.

"He's coming back," he said, and his voice sounded different as he looked over her head into the warehouse.

"Why is he leaving at all?"

Reese came back to the door. "Come on in. You're letting the heat out."

Trudy took a deep breath and stepped over the threshold into the warehouse, dragging Nolan with her since he wouldn't let go of her arm.

The place was a cavern filled with rows of shelving crammed with boxes, a giant version of the old toy store. High above, industrial lighting made the center space by the door bright, but the rest of the place was dark. It wasn't silent, though. There was a radio somewhere blaring "The Little Drummer Boy."

"Rum-pa-pum-pum," Trudy said, not at all reassured.

"Over here," Reese said, and led them away from the door, Trudy pulling Nolan along, since he still wouldn't let go. "You can leave your Mac here." He dropped his bag with the Twinkletoes in it. "I'm leaving my bag here."

"Where are the MacGuffins?" Trudy said, keeping a tight hold on her own bags.

"And who are *they*?" Nolan said, and Trudy looked back to see three men now standing in front of the door. They looked a lot like Reese, young and dudelike in denim jackets, but they weren't smiling.

Uh-oh, Trudy thought.

"Wait here," Reese said, and went over to confer with the men.

"You know, I don't feel good about this," she said to Nolan.

"Good instincts," Nolan said, not taking his eyes off the men. "Come here."

He tugged on her arm and she let him pull her over to the closest row of shelves.

"Be with you in a minute," Reese called back, and Trudy nodded to him, and then

Nolan jerked her arm and she tripped after him between two rows of shelves and into the darkness.

"What are you doing?" she said.

"Shhhh." He kept going, tugging her deeper into the gloom of the unlit shelving.

"What do you mean, 'Shhhh'? What's going on?"

"Quiet." Nolan pulled her down another side row and then across another one, effectively losing them both in the darkness.

"Stop shushing me. I don't like—"

He stopped and cupped her face with his hands and whispered, "Trudy, please shut up."

"Why?" Trudy whispered back.

He leaned closer and whispered in her ear. "Because I think Reese is a bad guy. And I think he wants your MacGuffin. And I think those guys out there are his minions. So we should—"

"Minions?" Trudy said, so startled she spoke out loud.

Nolan put his hand over her mouth. "And we don't want them to find us," he whispered. "Not unless you're prepared to give up that MacGuffin."

Trudy shook her head, and he took his hand away and bent to her ear again. "Then we should hide it here. They're going to find us, and we can tell them the box is here and let them spend the rest of their lives looking for it—"

Trudy shook her head again. *"No."*

He slapped his hand over her mouth and whispered, "*Listen.* I'm not a toy collector, I'm an undercover cop."

Trudy pulled back, trying to see him in the dark. "I don't believe it," she whispered back. "An undercover cop who teaches Chinese lit?"

"I'm a well-educated undercover cop."

"This is your explanation." She shook her head and started to move away, and he pulled her back.

"Look," he whispered in her ear, "we knew the bad guys were operating from the university lit department, and I really do have a degree in Chinese. And some literature. Hey, I'm a good teacher."

Actually, he was, Trudy remembered. That was another thing that had made her want to go out with him, competence. And now he was telling her that there was a toy-theft ring operating out of the lit department. "'The bad guys.' Is that really cop talk?"

"It's too dark to show you my ID. Want to feel my badge?"

"You have to be kidding me."

"Your buddy Reese—"

"He's not my buddy," Trudy said, and then

she heard Reese call her name from the center space of the warehouse and stepped closer to Nolan.

"Listen to me," Nolan said. "They're toy hijackers and they want that doll. If things get bad, *give it to them.*"

Toy hijackers? "No."

She heard him draw in his breath in exasperation, but she didn't care.

"This is for Leroy," she whispered. "His rat daddy ran off with the rat nanny, and his mother is in meltdown, but he knows Santa is bringing him a MacGuffin. He's getting it."

"Oh, Christ," Nolan said under his breath. "I'll get him another one, I swear. Just give them that one so we can walk out of here alive."

"That's not very heroic."

"I'll be heroic when you're not here," Nolan whispered. "Now I just want you out in one piece."

"I'm not giving up Leroy's Mac. What's your Plan B?"

Nolan sighed his exasperation and then took her arm and drew her deeper into the shelves. "We hide."

"Hide?" Trudy whispered back. "How—"

"Shut up," he whispered, and she did, following him deeper into the darkness until they came to a wall. He took her hand and led her along the wall until he found a staircase, and then he took her slowly up the stairs, testing each tread to make sure it didn't creak, which wasn't really necessary since "The Little Drummer Boy" had given way to Brenda Lee singing "Rockin' Around the Christmas Tree," making her usual Christmas fortune in residuals.

When they reached the top, they were on a walkway, looking out over the warehouse beneath the windows of a darkened office. Nolan tugged her arm and she sank down with him on the metal platform as silently as possible, her shopping bags rustling.

"Now what?" she whispered.

"Now we wait for backup."

"What backup?"

"The backup I sent the cabbie for. Shhhh."

He was peering over the rail, but they were too far away to see into the lighted part of the warehouse.

"You're really a cop?" Trudy whispered. "Why do I find that hard to believe?"

"I don't know," Nolan whispered back. "Why are you holding on to that damn doll when that could get us out of here?"

"What if you're not a cop? What if Reese is your accomplice and you're working together to get the Mac from me?"

"For our mutual nephew?" Nolan's whisper sounded a lot tougher now, but that might just have been the exasperation in his voice. "Has it occurred to you that you're trapped in a deserted warehouse with a bunch of thugs?"

"Yes," Trudy whispered back. "Well, no. For all I know, that's Reese's glee club out there. Maybe it's his bowling night. They're all wearing the same jacket."

"Be serious, Trudy. You're risking your life for a doll so your nephew won't be disappointed on Christmas Day in spite of the fact that his father is gone and his mother is in a gin coma."

"Hey."

"Shhhh. He's already disappointed, Tru. His family's gone. Give Reese the doll. When he makes a run for it, we'll arrest him. He won't get away with it."

Trudy pushed him away. "First, my sister is not in a gin coma. Second, his family is not gone; he has me and his mother when she sobers up. Third, if I give Reese this doll and you arrest him, the doll becomes evidence and I never see it again. So no. Leroy is going to get this doll tomorrow morning. He is going to believe in Santa, since he can't believe in men or nannies. When does your backup get here?"

"I don't think you can indict all men because of one Rat Daddy."

"Yeah? How many times have you lied to me tonight?"

Nolan leaned back against the wall. "Too

many to count. But I'm still here trying to save your cantankerous butt. That should mean something."

"I have only your word for that and as we know, you lie."

"Okay. We'll sit here and wait and hope Reese doesn't find us."

"That's your plan? Hope he doesn't find us?"

"You always this cranky?"

"Only when I'm cold, I'm tired, I'm scared, and men keep lying to me while I'm trying to get a kid the Christmas present he deserves."

"Okay, *fine*." Nolan shifted on the platform, his whisper savage in the darkness. "We'll take the doll if we can get out of here with it. Just promise me that if he says, 'The doll or your life,' you'll give him the doll."

"No."

"*Trudy*—"

"I can't." Trudy swallowed hard. "Leroy believes. Do you know how long it's been since I believed in anything? In anybody? But Leroy believes that when he comes downstairs tomorrow morning, there'll be a MacGuffin under his tree. He *knows* there will be because he believes in Santa Claus; he believes the world is a good place. And he's going to keep on believing that because I'm taking this doll home no matter what." She shifted against the cold wall. "Besides, nobody shoots anybody over a doll."

Nolan sighed. "I suppose it has occurred to you that you've lost your grip."

"No," Trudy said. "I've lost my faith. My grip is *just fine*." She pulled the shopping bags closer. "Leroy gets the Mac and Courtney gets the Twinkle, and then we'll put our lives back together."

"Their lives," Nolan said.

"Mine, too. My resolution for 2007 is to start believing in people again." She leaned closer to him. "I might start with you if you help me get this doll home."

He was quiet for a while. "Okay. I'll try to help you."

She pulled back. "I'll try to believe in you, then. No guarantees, of course."

"Okay, fine, I will help you," Nolan said.

"Promise me," Trudy said, gripping his coat. "Promise me that Leroy will have this Mac tomorrow morning."

"Trudy—"

"Fine." Trudy stood up, trying to keep her bags from rustling. "I'll do it myself. Could you move? I need to get past you to the stairs."

"I promise," Nolan said.

She looked down at him in the dark. "Easy to say."

"I promise," he said grimly, getting to his feet. "But now you have to do what I say."

"And why would I do that?" she said.

"Because you trust me."

"Ha."

"Then why are you listening to me?"

Trudy bit her lip. "I might trust you a little."

"All the way, Tru," Nolan said. "If I'm going to get you out of here, you have to do exactly what I say."

Trudy felt him close, his body warm next to hers in the darkness. If she was going to start trusting people, he might be the place to start. "You never even kissed me," she whispered. "What was that about? You never—"

He bent and kissed her, not gently, and she clutched at his jacket, wanting something to hold on to, putting her forehead against his shoulder when he broke the kiss because it had felt so right, everything about him felt so right.

The radio changed to "Grandma Got Run Over by a Reindeer."

Our song, Trudy thought. "Okay. I trust you. What do we do next?"

"Pray," Nolan said, sounding a little breathless. "Because we're in a world of hurt here."

"Well, then—"

Something moved behind him and Trudy saw one of the minions, just his face, for a second before Nolan jerked his elbow back and caught the guy across the nose. He turned and hit him again before he fell, catching him before he rolled off the platform. Trudy fumbled in her purse for her miniflash, but by the time she found it and turned it on, the guy was at Nolan's feet, his arms tied behind his back with a belt, and Nolan was putting on the guy's blue jacket.

"Turn that off," Nolan whispered, and Trudy did.

"So you're a cop," she whispered back.

"Here's the plan."

"How you did know where to hit him?" Trudy said. "It's dark as hell in here. How did you know?"

"You were looking at him," Nolan whispered back. "I hit what you were looking at. We have to move now; this guy found us and the others will, too. So I'm going down there to distract them. You're going out the door. If there's nobody out there yet, run for the street."

"I'm not leaving you," Trudy said, holding on to his sleeve.

"Trudy, I'm safer with you out of here than I am with you in here. You're a distraction. Now follow me until I get out into the light and they see me. Then run like hell for the door. Got it?"

She didn't want to leave him, that was wrong. But he was probably right, she wasn't going to be any help at all. "Okay."

"One more thing," Nolan said, and kissed

her, and this time it hit her hard, he was going out there to save her, and she kissed him back with everything she had.

When she came up for air, she was dizzy. "Maybe we should stay here," she whispered. "Hiding is good. We could do this until the backup shows."

"They'll come looking for this guy," Nolan whispered back, nodding to the minion at his feet. "We'll do this later." He looked at her, shook his head, and kissed her again, and she relaxed into him, irrationally happy about the whole mess.

Then he stepped back and she sighed.

"Right. Later," she said, and followed him down the stairs toward the light.

Nolan left her in the first row of shelves nearest the door, just steps away from the lighted part of the warehouse and the way out. "Watch until their backs are turned," he said. "Then run like hell."

She nodded, and he disappeared down the row again as her heart pounded.

He would be okay. Nobody killed over toys, even Major MacGuffins. They wouldn't do anything to him. She was almost sure. She bit her lip and waited, and then her cell phone rang and she grabbed it and answered it before it could ring again.

"Don't do that," she whispered into the phone.

"You didn't call me," Courtney said. "You're fifteen minutes late."

"Yeah, well there are guys after us," Trudy whispered.

"What guys?" Courtney said. *"What us?"*

"Nolan and me. Reese's got a ring of toy thieves here—"

"Toy thieves? What are you talking about?"

"Call nine-one-one," Trudy said, and then realized Courtney didn't know where they were. "We're—"

Somebody took her cell phone out of her hand, and she screamed and turned.

"Let's talk," Reese said, and shut off her phone.

"I'm not giving you the Mac," Trudy said, holding her bags behind her.

Reese sighed. "Trudy, I don't know what Nolan's told you, but I'm positive it's not the truth."

"He's a cop." Trudy took a step back. "And boy, are you in trouble."

"He's a double agent for the Chinese government," Reese said.

Trudy tightened her grip on her bags.

"Whoa. You've got a better imagination than he does. He said you were a toy thief."

Reese looked taken aback. "A toy thief? Who the hell steals toys?"

"The Grinch," Trudy said. "I don't know. It sounded plausible when he said it. It still sounds plausible compared to the Chinese-double-agent bit."

"I am not a toy thief," Reese said.

"But you don't have a nephew, either. Because we're in this warehouse and there are no Mac Twos, which means you had to get me here for some reason."

"The Chinese spy codes." Reese nodded toward her bags. "They're in that MacGuffin box. I'm with the CIA and I need them."

"Fat chance." Trudy stepped back again. "I don't care what alphabet you flash at me, you are not taking this Mac from me."

"Look on the box, Trudy," Reese said patiently. "In the lower right-hand corner, there should be a black X."

"There isn't," Trudy said, holding the bag tighter.

"It's small," Reese said. "Look for it."

Trudy hesitated, but he met her eyes without flinching. *He's telling the truth,* she thought, and put her bags down. She took the Mac box out of the bag and stepped into the light to look at it.

Sure enough, in the lower right-hand corner on the back was a small black *X*.

"You put it there," Trudy said, not wanting to believe Nolan was the bad guy.

"When?" Reese said. "You haven't let that box out of your hands since you got it."

"Oh, hell." Trudy swallowed. "I need this doll, Reese."

"It's okay," Reese said. "I don't need the doll. I just need the instruction sheet. That's where the codes are. Deal?"

Trudy bit her lip. Leroy didn't need the instructions; he probably knew more about the toy by now than the designers did. Toy hijackers and Chinese double agents were both ridiculous; Leroy was real. "Okay."

Reese held out his hand for the box, and she tightened her grip.

"Just the instructions." She opened the lid and felt down the back of the box for the paper, but there was nothing there. "Damn." She held the box into the pool of light cast by the fixture far above her and looked in. "It must have fallen under the doll." She carefully pulled the doll out, still wired into the cardboard backing that showed explosions, and shook the box upside down.

"Trudy," Reese said, his voice grim.

"I'm looking." Trudy dropped the empty

box to unwire the MacGuffin to see if the instructions had lodged behind it.

Reese picked up the box and began to dissemble it, checking in all the folds. "It's not here."

"It's not here, either." Trudy pulled the cardboard background away from the doll and handed it over, holding on to the Mac tightly. "And it was earlier."

"How do you know?"

"Because Nolan checked—" She stopped, appalled.

"Nolan opened the box and took out the instructions," Reese said, sounding grim.

"But he put them back, I saw him," Trudy said. "He slipped them behind the cardboard and closed up the box."

"He palmed them, Trudy. He got the codes."

Trudy thought back. "He couldn't have. I was watching him, right up to . . ."

Reese looked at her patiently.

"Right up to when you called to me in the checkout line," Trudy said, clutching the Mac closer and feeling miserable. "I looked away to talk to you. Did you see him take them?"

"No," Reese said. "I was looking at you."

Trudy felt ill. "Can I have the box back? At least I can give the doll to Leroy for Christmas." She bent, keeping the doll in one hand,

and picked up the shopping bags with the cow and the Twinkletoes in them.

"Look," Reese said. "I need your help. Nolan's a bad guy, and he's somewhere in this warehouse with those codes, and he trusts you. You call to him, get him to come out to us, and we'll take it from there."

Trudy stepped back. "You'll hurt him."

Reese shook his head, moving closer. "You watch too many movies. Spies don't hurt people, they just swap information. And that's all we're going to do. Take back the codes." He smiled at her, his baby face reassuring. "Just call out for him, Trudy. He'll come to you. He likes you. Then you can take the doll and go home, and you'll have done a good thing for your country, too." She hesitated and he said, "Of course, I'll have to check the doll before you go to make sure there's nothing else there." He held out his hand for the MacGuffin.

Of course you will, Trudy thought, and looked around him at the door. Could she shove him out of the way and get out?

"Come on," Reese said. "Who are you going to trust, me or the guy who lied to you and stole the instruction sheet?"

Good question.

She stuck the Mac under her arm, looped the two remaining shopping bags over her wrist, and opened her purse.

"Trudy?" Reese said.

"I'm gonna go with the guy who lied," Trudy said, and Maced him.

Reese had stopped screaming by the time Trudy found the staircase again, which comforted her some. If he was really a CIA agent, she'd just Maced a good guy, but on the other hand . . .

Actually, there wasn't an other hand. She'd just Maced a good guy.

"What the hell did you do to him?" Nolan whispered, and she jerked back, almost dropping her last two bags.

The Mac she kept her grip on.

"I Maced him. How'd you know I'd be here?"

"I figured this is where you'd run to once the other guys blocked the door. You were supposed to get out."

"Yeah, well, you were supposed to be the good guy," Trudy whispered back. "You took the instructions, you bastard."

"Yeah," Nolan said. "So?"

"So you're not a cop," Trudy said. "You're a double agent for the Chinese, you rat—"

"He *told* you that?"

Trudy stopped. "That is pretty far-fetched."

"Trudy, he's the double agent for the Chinese."

Trudy glared at where she thought he was in the darkness. "Do you guys just make this stuff up as you go?"

"MacGuffins are made in China," Nolan whispered. "They marked one box last year and sent it over to that toy store. We just found out that it went missing and never got picked up, which is why we had the toy store staked out."

"We who?" Trudy whispered back. "No, wait, I know this part. You're the CIA. And I'm pissed off. Do you really think I'm going to believe this crap? That the Chinese secret service puts codes in dolls? Why don't they just *e-mail* them?"

"Computers can be hacked."

"And Major MacGuffins can't?" Trudy looked at the doll in her arms.

"One sheet of paper, all the codes," Nolan said. "On microdot. Very efficient. Except they lost them last year."

"So this is about last year's codes?" Trudy shook her head. "Why would you want last year's codes? This story needs work."

"Because with last year's codes we can decipher all of last year's transmissions that we intercepted. Which is what's going on right now."

"Right now."

"I took them out of the box and passed them

on," Nolan said. "If you'll give the doll to Reese, he'll realize it's over and hit the road."

"Evidently not," Trudy said. "He knows you've got the instruction sheet and he doesn't seem to be leaving. I'm not buying any of this, you know. But I also don't care about any of it. As long as Leroy—"

"I know, I know, he gets the doll." Nolan sighed. "I can't believe I promised you that. I'm going to end up getting shot for some stupid doll."

"Yes, but you're saving a little boy's Christmas," Trudy said. "That's very heroic."

"I'm still gonna get shot," Nolan said. "So here's what we're going to do. You're going to take your Mace—"

"I dropped it," Trudy said.

"Great," Nolan said.

"Well, I never Maced anybody before. He scared the hell out of me when he screamed. But I'll be better now. And I don't need the Mace. I've seen *Miss Congeniality* twenty times, it's Courtney's favorite movie."

"What are you talking about?"

"That SING thing. Solar plexus, Instep, Nose, Groin."

"No." Nolan's whisper was flat in the darkness. "Do not think you're Rambo. Just run for the damn door."

"Okay." Trudy shifted the Mac to her other arm as she tried to remember what other weapons she might have in her purse. No Mace. No knife. No gun. She clearly hadn't come out prepared for Christmas Eve. Not even a nail file. . . . "Wait a minute." She reached in one of the bags, pulled out Courtney's Twinkletoes box, and pried the top open.

"What are you doing?" Nolan whispered.

"Arming myself." Trudy opened the manicure set wired next to Twink's feet. There was a nail file in there, just as she'd remembered. "Got it."

"Do not fight with anybody," Nolan whispered, the order clear. "Just run for the damn door."

"Okay." Trudy put the nail file in her coat pocket.

"We need something to create a disturbance. Too bad that grenade in the Mac doesn't work. I could use a grenade."

"There's a gun," Trudy brought up the Mac's hand so she could look down the barrel of the Mac's revolver. "What's this thing stuck on the end?"

"A silencer," Nolan whispered. "If only I had one for you."

"So is the gun louder with it off?"

"*Don't* fire that thing, we don't know what

it'll do." Nolan peered over the edge of the stairs.

Trudy leaned back against the staircase and looked at the gun. It was a horrible thing to give a kid. What were people thinking? Evil Nemesis Brandon's mother must have had a politically correct meltdown when she realized what was in the box, but she got it for him anyway. Well, good for ENB's mom. Trudy resisted the urge to pull the trigger and pulled on the silencer instead, which popped right off. "Whoops."

"Shhhh."

The silencer felt a little heavy for something that was basically a plastic cap. Trudy stuck her hand in her purse and found her miniflash. Hunching over to shield the light from the warehouse, she looked inside the cylinder. There was something rectangular stuck in there, about half an inch wide, with a slice of something white in it.

"Oh, hell," Trudy said out loud.

"Shhhh." Nolan turned on her. "You—"

"It's a thumb drive," Trudy whispered.

"What?"

"The silencer. It's a USB key, a thumb drive, you know, a mini hard drive. It wasn't just the code in the instructions—"

Nolan leaned in to look, and Trudy felt him

press warm against her as he took the silencer, his weight a comfort, especially since she knew she was holding something that Reese probably would shoot her for.

"This is not good," she whispered.

"Oh, honey, this is great," Nolan said in her ear. "Oh, babe, do you have any idea what you just found?"

"The thing Reese is going to kill me for?" Trudy said.

"He's not going to kill you," Nolan said, but he didn't sound as though he were giving the thought his full attention. "Give me that doll."

"No," Trudy said. "You can have the silencer, but you can't have—"

She heard something and shut up as Nolan froze.

Then he leaned forward and whispered in her ear, "I need your tape."

She frowned at him, and he began to go silently through her bags until he held up the Scotch tape she'd bought to wrap Leroy's Mac a million years ago. Then he put the gray plastic silencer on the underside of the gray railing along the wall and began to wrap tape around it.

Good thing I got the invisible kind, she thought, and wondered if she was ever going to get home.

"Okay," Nolan whispered when he was

done. "We're going out there again. And I will distract them and this time you will run for the door even if your phone rings."

"How are you going to distract them?"

"Give me that cow."

"The cow?" Trudy handed over the bag with the cow and hugged the Mac to her.

"You pull the string and it talks, right?"

"It says, 'Eat chicken.' "

"Right. Come on."

"Aren't you going to kiss me good-bye again?"

"No. I'm going with you this time."

"That's good, I like that better," Trudy said, and followed him down the stairs again, clutching the Mac and the Twinkletoes bag.

When they were back at the end of the row by the door, Nolan pulled the string and wrapped it around the cow's body. "Door's there," he whispered, nodding toward it.

She nodded back and gripped the nail file in her pocket while he drew his arm back.

"With your shield or on it, cow," he said, and tossed it over the shelves.

The string unwound itself before the cow cleared the top, and it mooed, "Eat chicken" as a fusillade rang out. Nolan shoved her toward the door, and she ran for it, hitting Reese, who was running around the end of the shelves, his eyes still red and streaming from the Mace as he raised his gun. He grabbed for her, and she stabbed him in the gun arm, dropping her Twinkletoes bag but still clutching the Mac as he screamed, and then she kicked him in the knee and ran like hell for the door, wrenching it open as Reese fired, hearing the bullet ping on the metal as she dove for the darkness.

Trudy ran for the edge of the parking lot, clutching the Mac, adrenaline pumping, not stopping when she heard, *"Hold it!"*

Somebody grabbed Trudy's arm and swung her around and she saw it was the cabdriver. *"Give me that doll,"* he said.

"No." She smacked him with the bag and as he raised one hand to protect his head, she saw the gun in the shoulder holster under his leather jacket.

"Damn it," she said, and swung her elbow sharply into his solar plexus, stamped down on his instep, punched him in the nose, and then tried to kick him in the groin and missed and got his thigh instead, collapsing him onto the pavement.

Good enough, she thought, and took off for the street, only to have somebody else grab her arm just as she reached the chain-link fence.

"No," she said, and tried to turn, but who-

ever it was wrapped his other arm around her waist and pulled her back against him.

"Stop it!" Nolan said. "It's me. Give me the Mac."

"*No*," Trudy said, furious, and smacked her head back into his nose. She heard him swear and knew she'd gotten him, but he didn't let go, so she tried for his instep, but he jerked her off her feet.

"*Trudy, stop it.*"

She swung her elbow back again and missed, and he kicked her feet out from under her and dumped her onto the grimy, wet pavement, yanking her arms behind her.

"You couldn't make this easy, could you?" he said as her cheek scraped on the ground. "You had to be a hard-ass."

"*You bastard, you promised me I'd keep the doll,*" she said, and then she felt him yank her wrists together as he slapped handcuffs on her and took the Mac away from her.

"Trudy Maxwell. You've been taken into custody for criminal obstinacy."

"Fuck you," Trudy said into the pavement. "And you have to be an actual cop to take me into custody, which you are not, so don't think I'm not going to sue your ass for kidnapping."

He put his arm under her and lifted her gently back onto her feet. "I'm not kidnapping you."

"Yeah?" Her hair fell in her eyes and she couldn't brush it out, which made her madder. "You and Reese, this was all a setup. He didn't even shoot at you back there, he shot at me. You were working together."

Nolan swung her around and gave her a gentle push back toward the warehouse. There were more cars there now and a van, and while she watched, somebody shoved Reese into the back of one of the cars. He was handcuffed.

"Not working with Reese," Nolan said.

"I don't see any police department insignia on these cars," Trudy said, shrugging off his hand as he prodded her forward. "In fact, I don't see any insignia at all."

Nolan stopped her in the pool of light from one of the warehouse lamps and showed her his ID.

"'NSA,'" Trudy read. "Very cute. Got one for the CIA and the FBI, too? How about FEMA, I hear they're really tough. Not as tough as double agents for the Chinese, of course. How dumb do you think I am?"

"Trudy, I am NSA, Reese was a double agent for the Chinese, and I really did try to help you."

"Yeah," Trudy said bitterly. "That's why I'm in handcuffs now."

"You're in handcuffs because you're resisting," Nolan said. "I'm trying to get a promotion here, and you're beating me up. It makes me look bad."

"Great. That's what this is about, some damn promotion? Knock a helpless woman to the ground and steal her little nephew's Christmas present?"

"The 'helpless' is debatable," Nolan said as they went past the cabbie, who was dabbing at his bleeding nose and glaring at her. "You owe Alex an apology."

"He attacked me."

"He was trying to get you into the cab so he could get you away from here," Nolan said. "He's one of ours."

"He was trying to take the doll, so he's not one of mine," Trudy said, and then she saw the woman they were moving toward. She was wearing a red and green bobble hat, but she didn't look like a Christmas shopper anymore. "Who the hell is she?"

"My boss," Nolan said.

Trudy waited until they were in front of the woman, and then she said, "Is this guy really an NSA agent?"

"Yes." The woman spoke without any expression whatsoever, which only made Trudy madder.

"Well, he groped me in that warehouse," Trudy said.

"I'm not at all surprised," the woman said, and held her hand out for the Mac.

Nolan gave it to her.

"You *bastard*," Trudy said.

"Trudy, it's national security."

"No, it isn't," Trudy snapped. "You got the codes when you got the instruction sheet, and then you got the USB key when you got the silencer. You don't need the doll. You don't care that a little kid is going to wake up tomorrow and know that everything in his world is a lie, that doesn't bother you—"

"Trudy," Nolan said, misery in his voice.

"—as long as your *work* gets done." She wrenched away from him, her hands still cuffed behind her. "You guys, guys like you and Reese and Prescott, you don't care about anything as long as you get what you want. Well, *fine*, you got it. Now take these handcuffs off me, because you know damn well you're not going to arrest me for anything."

"You have to promise to stop hitting people," Nolan said.

"Fine," Trudy said. "I promise."

He unlocked the cuffs and she kicked him in the shin. He said, "Ouch," and grabbed at his leg.

"You promised me," Trudy said. "You said I could trust you, and I was as dumb as Courtney, I believed you." She turned back to his boss. "You need me for anything else or can I go home to my devastated family?"

"We have questions," the woman said, and gestured to the car. "We'll have you home in a couple of hours."

"Fine," Trudy said, refusing to look back at Nolan. "I'll tell you anything you want as long as you give me back the Mac."

"Unfortunately not," the woman said.

"Here's your Twinkletoes," Nolan said, holding out a shopping bag. "I found it in the warehouse."

Trudy took the bag. "Rot and die," she said, and walked toward the car.

"Trudy, be reasonable," he said, following her. "This is *national security*—"

She turned around and he almost bumped into her. "You didn't have to kiss me and tell me I could trust you. You didn't have to make me believe in you again. You had the NSA out here, you were always going to get that damn doll. You could have left me my dignity, but no, you had to sucker me in."

"That's not fair."

She stepped closer. "That's why I hate you. That's why Leroy's going to hate his dad and his mom and me tomorrow, because he knew there was no Santa, but we all said, 'Trust us,

Santa's gonna come through for you.' We hung that kid out to dry. He's going to be right to hate us. And I'm right to hate you."

She turned to get into the car, and he caught her arm and said, "Trudy, I'm sorry," and she shook him off and got into the backseat without looking back at him.

Chapter 3

Trudy borrowed a cell phone and called Courtney to tell her she was all right. Then she faced Nolan's boss, who ditched the hat with the green and red bobbles and became tough, efficient, thorough, and polite, none of which made Trudy feel better. She answered everything the woman asked, and when she was finally released it was well after midnight. She took her purse and the battered bag with the Twinkletoes and rode home through the snow in the back of a black car, too tired and too defeated to argue anymore.

I couldn't do it alone, she thought. *I really needed that bastard's help; nobody could have done it alone.* But she still felt like a failure. If only she hadn't trusted him, hadn't trusted Reese, hadn't gotten in that cab in the first place, hadn't ever talked to Nolan at all, they'd never have known she'd found the MacGuffin and Leroy would have it now. Her throat swelled and she stared at the back of the driver's head and willed herself not to cry. Not in front of the NSA, anyway.

She tiptoed into the house, but Courtney called out from the dimly lit living room. Trudy went in and found her on the couch, glass in hand, her feet propped up on the coffee table that held a bowl of white icing, a lopsided gingerbread house, and a stack of gingerbread men with a knife stuck through them. She was staring into the gas fire, and the glow reflected off the tinsel on the tree while Christmas music played low and slow in the background.

"Do you have it?" Courtney said, her voice dull.

"No." Trudy went around the mess on the coffee table and sat down beside her, dropping her bags on the floor. "The Feds took it from me. For national security reasons. Nice gingerbread house."

"It's crooked," Courtney said, clearly not caring. "The Feds?"

"Turns out Nolan works for the NSA. I know. Unbelievable."

"I believe it." Courtney sat unmoving, her eyes on the fire. "That's just my luck. Even the government is out to get me."

"Two governments. Reese the Surfer turned out to be a double agent for the Chinese." Trudy leaned forward, pulled the knife out of the gingerbread, and scooped up a glop of white icing.

"Well, at least you're meeting men." Courtney picked up her glass to drink and then made a face when she realized it was empty. "So why did they want the Mac?"

"It had the codes to the Chinese spy network on the instruction sheet and then something else was on this thumb drive disguised as a silencer for the gun." Trudy smeared the icing on the roof. The white mass hung there for a moment and then began to slump its way to the edge. Not enough powdered sugar. The icing plopped off onto the cardboard base, looking like a snowbank.

"Chinese spy codes?" Courtney said.

"I wouldn't have believed it, except that I saw the thumb drive. That and there were so many guys in bad black suits there at the end." She glopped more icing on the other side of the roof. It slumped and became a snowbank, too. Definitely too thin. "Where's the sugar, Court?"

Courtney gestured to the kitchen with her glass.

The kitchen looked like a war zone, bodies of mutilated gingerbread men everywhere, red and green gumdrops stuck to the island like body parts, and a drip of icing pooled on the floor like thick white blood.

"Christmas didn't used to be this violent," Trudy called back to Courtney, and then picked up the powdered-sugar box, the half-filled bag of gumdrops, and some toothpicks. Toothpicks were good. She could probably have done more damage in the warehouse if she'd had toothpicks. She could have stuck several of them into Reese.

And more into Nolan. *Nolan,* she thought, and blinked back tears. *Damn.*

She went back to the living room. Courtney hadn't moved.

Trudy dumped her armload on the coffee table and sat down beside Courtney. "Forget about rotten men. There was one good thing that happened tonight. I got you a present."

Courtney turned her head a millimeter. "Does it have gin in it?"

"No, but you want it anyway." Trudy pulled the Twinkletoes box out of her last shopping bag and handed it to Courtney, who stared at it for a moment, her eyes unfocused.

Then she sat up slowly, her forehead smoothing out, her lips parting. "Where—"

"They're making them again. Like a reissue. Second chance. Do-over."

"Oh, please," Courtney said, but she said it while she was ripping the cellophane off the package. She pried open the top and pulled out the cardboard shell with the Twinkletoes doll and her manicure set wired to it. "These aren't the same colors of polish as the old one."

"I'm sorry—"

"These are better." Courtney began to unwire the doll. "She has really big feet."

"Well, she needs really big toenails if little kids are going to paint them." Trudy watched her for a minute and then went back to the gingerbread house as Courtney set up her play station. One thing had gone right that evening, she thought as she beat sugar into the thickening icing. Now if she could get the icing and the gumdrop shingles to stay on the iced roof, that would be two. It was tomorrow morning that was going to be bad.

Poor Leroy.

Damn it.

She began to spackle the roof with the thicker icing, thinking vicious thoughts about government agents who took toys from little kids on Christmas. She picked up a red gumdrop and shoved it into the icing with more force than necessary and almost cracked the roof.

Easy, she told herself and looked back at Courtney, who was studying the Twinkletoes doll with an odd expression on her face.

Well, she was drunk.

Trudy shoved another gumdrop into the icing and dared it to fall off. It didn't.

At least Leroy would have a gingerbread house in the morning. That might help calm things down. She filled in rows of red gumdrop shingles, trying to think of things to say to him.

"Sorry about your Mac, Leroy, but Santa sent you this nice toy cow instead."

No, they'd shot the cow. Jesus.

"Santa got delayed over Pittsburgh but he's going to put your Mac on backorder."

No, Santa was not a mail-order house.

"Maybe it fell off the sleigh."

Trudy shoved another gumdrop in. *Bastards.*

Not that Leroy would throw a fit. He wasn't a fit-throwing kind of kid. But he'd be disappointed; that stillness would be on his face, like the stillness that had been there when his father left.

Men, she thought, and shoved in another gumdrop, but that wasn't fair, she knew it wasn't fair. Nolan had risked his life for her at the end. Maybe even before the end, maybe that was why he'd gotten in the cab, because he cared. Trudy sat up a little. "You know, I think he came along in the cab to save me."

Courtney had the doll out now and her shoes off. "Who?"

"Nolan." Trudy watched Courtney pry open the bottle of silver nail polish, awake and alert, if still a little unsteady from the booze. "He took the Mac away from me at the end after he'd sworn to me he wouldn't, but when he got in the cab at the toy store, he thought he already had the codes. He didn't need me anymore. Maybe he got in to protect me from Reese." She put the last gumdrop on the roof gently. Maybe Nolan cared about her, at least as much as he cared about the Mac.

She looked closer at the roof. The gumdrops seemed to be sliding down.

Beside her, Courtney painted the first Twinkle toe, her face concentrating on the job. Court didn't look particularly happy, but she did look alert. That was something. Trudy picked up a green gumdrop and flattened it and then threaded it onto a toothpick, the first set of branches for a gumdrop tree.

Okay, so Nolan worked for the NSA. Well, good for him, protecting his country. And of course he had to lie to her about his name, he was undercover.

And if he'd gotten into that cab without needing to, if he'd gotten in with her to save her, then maybe he was a good guy. She flattened another gumdrop onto the toothpick and then paid attention for the first time to the music in the background, a slow growly voice singing, "Hurry down the chimney tonight."

She looked at Courtney, jolted out of her fairy tale. "Is that 'Santa Baby'?"

Courtney nodded as she finished Twinkle's last toe. "Yeah. I couldn't get it out of my head after you talked about it."

Trudy listened to the slow, jazzy version on Court's stereo. "That is not Madonna."

"Etta James," Courtney said. "The only good thing I know about Pres is his taste in music. And his kid." She screwed the top back on the polish and looked at the doll, her pretty face puzzled.

"What's wrong?"

"This is a dumb toy." Courtney turned Twinkle around so Trudy could see her vapid plastic face.

Trudy sighed and stuck the last green gumdrop on the top of the toothpick. "I always thought so, but then I wasn't the manicure type. You probably would have loved it when you were six." *Timing is everything. If Nolan already knew all he needed to about the codes when he got in my cab—*

"No, it would have been a huge letdown then, too." Courtney set the doll on the table, where its pink party dress flopped into the icing. "I'm sure there's a lesson in this, but I'll be damned if I know what it is."

"I know what you mean." Trudy stuck her gumdrop tree into the gingerbread beside the door. The red gumdrop shingles had moved another millimeter. "I'd love to find a meaning for what happened tonight besides 'Don't trust men,' but I don't think there is one." *Except maybe Nolan came with me to keep me safe.*

"You don't know that yet." Courtney picked up the manicure set and unzipped it. "The doll was a letdown, but this could be a really great manicure set. You have to believe."

"Do you really think so?" Trudy said, trying not to sound hopeful.

"No. But I think that's what I'm supposed to say." Courtney opened the pink plastic manicure set. "And this is not a great manicure set."

"Oh, sorry," Trudy said. "I used the nail file to stab somebody, so it's gone."

"No, it's in here." Courtney held the case so she could see in. "It looks like it's in pretty good shape. No blood."

Trudy straightened. "It shouldn't be in there at all. The last time I saw it, it was stuck in Reese."

"Must have been a different box." Courtney took the file out. "This box was kind of mushed in the back. Did you—"

Trudy took the box and turned it over. The bottom corner was smashed, as if somebody had driven it into a counter, and over the creases was marked a tiny black X.

Oh no, she thought as her hope deflated. This was why Reese had been in the toy store; he'd been picking up this year's codes. And that was why Nolan had gotten in the cab: he hadn't been trying to save her, he'd been following Reese and the Twinkletoes. More Chinese codes, not her. *You're so dumb,* she told herself. *He betrays you and you still want to believe.*

"What?" Courtney said.

"Nolan picked up the wrong Twinkletoes box in the warehouse. He got Reese's instead of mine." Trudy pulled out the instruction sheet. "He wanted this." She stared at the flimsy paper with its bad illustration of Twinkle and its warning not to drink the nail polish in both

Chinese and English. "I bet this is this year's codes." She looked over at Courtney holding the neon pink nail file. "Let me see that, please."

Courtney handed over the file, its thick pink plastic handle first. Trudy grabbed the file end and yanked on the handle until it came apart.

"What are you doing?'

"It's a thumb drive," Trudy said when she was sure it was. She showed the end to Courtney. "More espionage stuff. Nolan saw Reese leave the store with a Twinkle, but I had one, too. He got the two bags mixed up in the warehouse and gave me the one with the codes by mistake."

"What does that mean?" Courtney said.

Trudy felt like throwing up. "It means that he's going to show up here and take your Twinkletoes away."

Courtney sat back. "That's okay. It's lousy nail polish, too."

"Another dream shattered," Trudy said, trying to make it sound like a joke.

"Twinkle or Nolan?"

"Both." Trudy packed up the box, feeling sick and stupid.

"Gin?" Courtney picked up her glass.

Trudy shook her head. "You know how dumb I am? I'm so dumb, I believed in that bastard even though I knew he'd lied to me. I even believed he got in that cab to save me. That's how much I wanted to believe."

"He did save you at the end."

"To get the doll," Trudy said, miserable. "And now I'm alone and Leroy is not getting a MacGuffin. So how dumb am I?"

"You're not dumb."

Trudy sank back into the couch as Etta began to sing "Have Yourself a Merry Little Christmas." "Because you know what? I still want to see him. He took my MacGuffin and I still want to see him. I want to *kill* him, but I want to see him."

Courtney nodded in sympathy. "I know. I hate Pres but I'd take him back. That's so sad."

"Prescott will come back," Trudy said tiredly. "When the novelty wears off, he'll want his nice home and his cute kid and his pretty wife again." *And I hope you slam the door in his face because that's what I'm going to do when Nolan comes after this doll.*

Courtney shook her head. "Forget Pres. Tell me about Nolan. Did he say, 'I'll call you'? What was the last thing he said?"

"He said, 'I'm really sorry'," Trudy said, remembering the miserable look on his face at the end. That had been something: he knew he'd screwed her over.

"And what did you say?"

"I think it was, 'Rot and die.' "

"You think you might have been overreacting there?"

"No." Trudy sat up again and stuck another red gumdrop on the roof of the gingerbread house. "I think I just told him the truth. Which was the best thing I could have done. I don't care if he thinks I'm nuts or irrational or anything else, I told him the truth. He did the worst possible thing he could do to me, so don't bother showing up with flowers, making cute apologies and bad jokes. And yes, I know it's not all about him, I know he's cashing Daddy's emotional checks, but right now? It's about him."

"He sounded like a nice guy when you were dating him."

"He is. He's great. Hell, Dad's a nice guy most of the time. That's why we believed in him for so long. He loved us, he was a good guy, how could he keep forgetting us like that? Jesus, Courtney, I could have ended up in a relationship like that. 'Nolan's a nice guy, he loves me, why am I bleeding from the ears all the time?' "

Courtney nodded. "Yeah. I know. It was almost a relief when Pres left because I could finally stop aching with disappointment." She sighed. "Except there's Leroy. Now I ache for Leroy. Especially tomorrow morning."

"We did it to him, you know." Trudy blinked back tears. "We should have said, 'Leroy, there is no Santa, and there's not going to be a Mac Two under the tree on Christmas Day, although we will do whatever we have to do to get you one as soon as possible because we love you and always will.' We should have told him the truth. Hell, Evil Nemesis Brandon told him the truth. Pretty damn bad when the only person you can trust is your Evil Nemesis." *You and me, Leroy.*

"I hate the truth. Except this part." Courtney gestured to the Twinkletoes box. "The part where you almost got yourself killed trying to get him that MacGuffin. The part where you brought me a Twinkletoes to make up for twenty years ago. The part where you're fixing my gingerbread house. The part where we'll take care of Leroy together tomorrow. I like that part of the truth."

Trudy dropped the gumdrops and sat back next to her sister, and Courtney snuggled closer and put her head on Trudy's shoulder.

"Yeah," Trudy said, patting her arm. "I like the part where you waited up for me. And did the boring part of the gingerbread house. And didn't tell me I'm an idiot for still wanting a lying bastard."

"So it's not so bad," Courtney said as the first gumdrop slid off the roof of the gingerbread house.

They watched for a minute while another slowly followed the first one.

Trudy thought about putting them back again and decided to let them slide. "What are we going to tell Leroy tomorrow?"

"How about, 'Maybe it fell off the sleigh'?" Courtney said.

Trudy sighed. "Well, it beats, 'Aunt Trudy had a Mac for you, but the United States government lied to her and took it away.' "

"Yeah," Courtney said. "He's mature for his age, but we'd never be able to explain that one. I'm still not sure I get it."

"That's okay." Trudy straightened. "I get it. Let's go to bed."

She stood up and pulled Courtney to her feet and steered her in the direction of the stairs, and when her sister was gone she walked around shutting off lights and turning off the fire, stopping when she came to the stereo where the CD had changed. Judy Garland was singing "Have Yourself a Merry Little Christmas," the carol that most made Trudy want to kill herself every holiday. She stood in the darkness and listened to Judy break her heart and let the tears drip as she thought of Leroy in the morning and of Nolan that night. *I really did believe in you,* she thought. *For about five minutes, I believed, and it felt really good.*

Then Judy finished her song and Trudy turned the stereo off and went to bed.

• • •

The next morning, Trudy curled up in an armchair in her flannel robe and mainlined coffee while Leroy opened his presents. When he was done, he turned and looked at them, standing straight in his Lilo and Stitch footie PJs, and said, " 'Guffin?"

Courtney swallowed. "It wasn't in there? Gee, baby, maybe it fell off the sleigh."

Leroy looked at her with the five-year-old version of, *How dumb do you think I am?*

Trudy put her coffee cup down and took a deep breath. "Leroy, here's the thing. There really isn't a—"

The doorbell rang, and she stopped, grateful for any interruption. "I'll get it." She went to the front door and looked through the square windows at the top, through the gold wreath Courtney had hung on the outside.

Nolan was standing there, looking like three kinds of hell.

Good, she thought, *you're as miserable as I am,* and opened the door. "Oh, look, it's a Christmas miracle."

He was holding two Christmas gift bags, slumping with exhaustion as the snow started to settle on his thick, dark hair. "Merry Christmas, Trudy."

"Ho ho ho," Trudy said. "I was just about to

explain to my five-year-old nephew that there is no Santa. Can you come back at another time? Never would be good for me."

He held out one of the bags. "Chill on the Santa. I got you covered."

"Uh huh," Trudy said.

"Go ahead. Look."

She took the bag and looked inside at the top of a camo-colored box that said, *New! Now with Toxic Waste!* "You are kidding me." She pulled out the box and saw the Mac Two, its pudgy little face uglier than ever now that its lips were pursed to spit goop. "How—"

"Top-secret," Nolan said, trying an exhausted smile on her. "I'd tell you, but then I'd have to kill you."

"That's lame." She put the Mac Two back in the bag, hope beginning to rise that maybe he wasn't a rat until she remembered that what he'd really come for was the Twinkletoes. She handed the bag back to him. "You're too late. And your patter is falling off."

"It's six A.M., I've had no sleep, and I'm freezing." Nolan held the bag out to her again. "Everything I have is falling off. Will you take this, please?" Then he looked past her, toward the floor, and said, "Hi."

Trudy turned to see Leroy, blinking up at them, looking absurdly small in his footie pajamas.

"What's that?" Leroy said, pointing to the Christmas bag.

"I found it out on the front lawn," Nolan said. "I think it fell off the sleigh." He handed it to Leroy.

Leroy looked into the top of it and his face lit up. *"Mom!"* he yelled. "You were *right*!" He took off for the living room and then stopped and came back. "Thank you very much for finding my 'Guffin," he said to Nolan, and then took off for the living room again, so happy that Trudy felt her throat close.

"Cute kid," Nolan said, and looked back at Trudy.

"Thank you," she said, feeling absurdly relieved. *Don't get suckered by this guy again.* "Well, I'd invite you in, but I'm still mad at you. So thanks. Merry Christmas. Have a good life. Somewhere else." She shut the door in his face.

"If you don't sleep with him, I will," Courtney said from behind her. "He got my kid a *MacGuffin*. He forgot the extra toxic waste, but what the hell."

"He's not leaving," Trudy said as the doorbell rang again. "Go get your Twinkletoes, he's going to ask for it next." She opened the door.

"Forgot this." Nolan handed her three packages of toxic waste.

"How do you feel about dating women with children?" Courtney said.

"Get the Twinkletoes," Trudy said, and Courtney went back to the living room.

Nolan leaned in the doorway, looking too tired to stand. "Look, I know you're mad, and I don't blame you, but I want to see you again. We got off to a bad start because we were lying to each other—"

"I never lied to you," Trudy said, outraged.

"You like faculty cocktail parties? And you really wanted to see that foreign film I took you to?"

"I was trying to help you," Trudy said. "I was trying to fit into your world."

"You were boring as hell," Nolan said.

"Hey!"

"But not last night. Last night you were somebody I want to see again. Without the violence."

Trudy leaned in the other side of the doorway, watching the snow swirl behind him. "You know, if I didn't know what I do know, I'd be pretty happy with that speech. But I know what you came for. Tell me the truth and you can have it. And then you can go away forever."

"If I'm going away forever, I'm not getting what I want," Nolan said.

"Funny," Trudy said. "Okay, play your stupid game. Courtney's getting the doll."

"What doll?" Nolan said.

"The one with the smashed-in corner and

the X. Like the MacGuffin. Only this year it's the Twinkletoe—" She stopped as Nolan's face changed from exhausted to alert.

"Let me see it," he said, and stepped inside, pushing her in front of him and closing the door behind him as Courtney came into the hall with the box.

"Hi. I'm Courtney, Trudy's sister." Courtney handed him the Twinkletoes.

"Nice to meet you, Courtney." Nolan took the box.

"The instructions are in there," Trudy said, a little uncertain now. "The USB key is in the nail file this time."

"You are kidding me." Nolan opened the box and took out the manicure set. Then he tucked the box under one arm, took out the nail file, and yanked the handle off. "You're not kidding me," he said, looking at the end of the USB key. "I will be damned." He put the file back in the case and the case back in the box. "I have to make a call. You stay here." He went back out onto the porch, shutting the door behind him.

"Thanks, I will," Trudy said to the door.

He hadn't known about the Twinkletoes.

Courtney went up on tiptoe to see out the little windows. "He's on his cell phone."

"Yeah?" Trudy said.

He really hadn't known about the Twinkletoes.

Courtney sank back on her heels. "He didn't know about the Twinkletoes, Tru. I think he's a good one. Plus he's hot."

"Maybe," Trudy said, and then the doorbell rang again.

"I'll just go see what my son is doing with his new tac nuke," Courtney said, and went back into the living room.

Trudy took a deep breath and opened the door.

"The thanks of a grateful nation are yours," Nolan said, meeting her eyes and taking her breath away. "Now about us."

"Us?" Trudy said, her voice cracking.

"Yeah, us. I know I really screwed you over last night."

"Well, national security and all," Trudy said.

He really hadn't known about the codes in the Twinkletoes.

"But I keep my promises," Nolan said, his eyes steady on hers.

"Good for you," Trudy said.

He hadn't known.

"I said you'd have this on Christmas morning." Nolan held out the other bag. "I know it's a mess, but . . ."

Trudy took the bag and looked inside. "What the . . ." She pulled out the Mac One. The box was gone, and the doll was battered and mangled, but it was her Mac. She squeezed it, and it made a crackly sound. "What did you do to it?"

"They had to take a code machine out of it," Nolan said. "So I got some paper from the paper shredder and restuffed it."

Trudy pulled up the Mac's jacket to see a broad band of duct tape wound around its belly. "Duct tape."

"I don't sew," Nolan said. "Besides, duct tape is better. It's a guy thing."

Trudy smoothed the little camo shirt back down and tried to rub the smudge of dirt off the Mac's nose. He looked nicer now, she thought, all ripped up and eviscerated and dirty. More vulnerable. Plus one of his eyebrows had come off, so now he just looked half-mad. *Kind of like me.*

"Reese threw the box away in the warehouse," Nolan went on. "I looked but couldn't find it. The silencer was the thumb drive, so that has to stay with NSA. They think the ammo belt may have something in it, too. And his boots—"

"How did you ever talk them into letting you take the doll?" Trudy said, amazed.

"I didn't give them much choice," Nolan said. "My future was riding on it."

Trudy blinked up at him.

"You know. Assuming you're ever going to talk to me again."

"You got in the cab thinking you already had the codes, didn't you?" Trudy said. "Did the NSA tell you to do that?"

"No, they told me to stay put since they had the cab under control."

"Why'd you get in?"

Nolan shrugged. "I wasn't that sure they had it under control."

"You came along to protect me," Trudy said.

"Yeah," Nolan said. "But don't go giving me any medals because that turned out great for me. We ended up with everything we needed because I got in that cab. Following you around made me look like a genius to my boss." He shook his head. "And now we have this year's codes. You're good for me, Gertrude."

Trudy wrapped her arms around the Mac, feeling the crunch of its duct tape against her stomach. "You turned out pretty good for me, too, Nolan."

He nodded and met her eyes for a long moment.

Kiss me, she thought.

Then he said, "I have to go."

"Of course," Trudy said, deflating.

"But I would like to come back," he said, as if he were choosing his words very carefully. "Can I have you, uh"—he shook his head—"see you later tonight?"

Under the Christmas tree with all the lights on. "Yes," Trudy said primly. "That would be very nice." *Kiss me.*

"Okay then." Nolan looked at a loss for words. "About seven?"

"Seven is good," Trudy said. *Kiss me.*

"I'll see you at seven then," Nolan said. "I really will, I promise."

"I believe you," Trudy said. "Thank you for the MacGuffin." *Kiss me, you idiot.*

"Uh, you're welcome. Thank you for the Chinese spy codes." He turned to go.

"Wait," Trudy said, and when he turned back she grabbed the lapel of his coat and pulled him down to her and kissed him good, and he dropped the Twinkletoes and pulled her close, squashing the Mac One between them.

"I'm crazy about you," he whispered when he broke the kiss.

"I'm crazy about you, too," she said, dizzy with happiness. "Hurry back."

"I will," he said fervently, and then he was gone, off into the snow, but he'd be back. He'd promised, and she believed him.

She closed the door and went back into the living room just in time to see Leroy squeeze the Mac Two so that green toxic waste shot across the room as Madonna sang "Santa

Baby" on the radio and Courtney dipped a broken gingerbread arm into her gin.

"I love Christmas," Trudy said, and went to join her family.

Christmas Bonus

Lori Foster

Chapter 1

Eric Bragg heard the even staccato clicking of her designer high heels coming down the polished hallway. He straightened in his chair as anticipation thrummed through him, matching the quickened beat of his heart.

He knew the sound of Maggie's long-legged, purposeful walk with an innate awareness that exemplified his growing obsession with her.

He could easily identify the sound of her stride apart from that of all the other employees. Mostly because when he heard it, he felt the familiar hot need, mixed with disgruntled dismay, that always seemed to be a part of him these days wherever Maggie Carmichael was concerned.

He remembered a time not too long ago when her footsteps would have been muted with sneakers that perfectly matched her tattered jeans and oversized sweatshirts. A time when she was so anxious to visit the office, she wouldn't have bothered to measure her stride and she would have forgotten her now-impeccable good manners in her excitement at the visit. She used to hurry up and down the hallways with all the enthusiasm of a nineteen-year-old woman-child, almost old enough, almost mature enough.

Eric shifted, trying to settle himself more comfortably in his large chair while his muscles tightened and his pulse quickened.

Unfortunately for Eric, Maggie had stepped right out of college and into the role of boss, a circumstance he had never foreseen. Perhaps if he had, he wouldn't have bided his time so patiently, waiting for the differences in their ages to melt away under the influence of experience and maturity. Ten years wasn't much, he'd always told himself, unless you were tampering with an innocent daydreamer still in college. *The boss's daughter—and now the damn boss.*

But who would have guessed that her father would pass away so unexpectedly from a stroke? Or that he would have left Maggie, fresh-faced and uncertain, in charge of his small but growing company, rather than Eric, who'd served as his right-hand man for many years?

Deliberately, Eric loosened his hold on the pen he'd been using to check off items on a new supply order and placed it gently on his cluttered desk. Every other year, at just about this time, Maggie had visited him. She'd be out of school on Christmas break and she'd show up wearing small brass bells everywhere. They used to be tied in the laces of her shoes, hanging from a festive bow in her long, sinfully sexy hair, on ribbons around her neck. She loved Christmas and decorating and buying gifts. Eric reached into his pocket and smoothed his thumb over the engraved key ring she'd given him the year before.

This year, everything was different. *This year, he'd become her employee.*

Sprawled out in his seat, pretending a comfort he didn't feel, Eric waited for her. But still, he caught his breath as Maggie opened his door without knocking and stepped in.

There wasn't a single bell on her person. No

red velvet ribbons, no blinking Santa pins. She was so damn subdued these days, it was almost as if the old Maggie had never existed. The combination of losing her father and gaining the responsibility of a company had changed her. Her glossy black hair had long since been cut into a chic shorter style, hanging just to the tops of her breasts. When she'd first cut it, he'd gotten rip-roaring drunk in mourning the loss of a longtime fantasy. Her slender body, which he'd become accustomed to seeing in sporty, casual clothes, was lost as well, beneath a ridiculously boxy, businesslike suit. It was drab in both color and form—but it still turned him on.

He knew what was beneath that absurd armor she now wore, knew the slight, feminine body that it hid.

And her legs . . . oh, yeah, he approved of the high heels Maggie had taken to wearing. They'd helped him to contrive new fantasies, which he utilized every damn night with the finesse of a masochist, torturing himself while wondering about things he'd likely never know. He went to sleep thinking about her, and woke up wanting her.

He was getting real used to surviving with a semi-erection throughout the day.

He felt like a teenager, once again caught in the heated throes of puberty. Only now, groping a girl in the backseat of his car wasn't about to put an end to his aching. Hell, an all-night sexual binge with triplets wouldn't do the trick. He wanted only Maggie, naked, hot, breathless, accepting him and begging him and . . .

Damn, but he had to get a grip!

"Maggie." He ignored the raw edge to his voice and eyed her still features as she stared at him. There was a heated quality to her gaze, as if she'd read his thoughts. "You're flushed, hon. Anything wrong?"

Maggie looked him over quickly, her large brown eyes widening just a bit as her gaze coasted from the top of his head to the toes of his shoes. Unlike Maggie, he hadn't trussed himself up in a restricting suit. But then, he never had. From the day he'd been hired, he'd made do with comfortable corduroy slacks or khakis—a true concession from his preference of jeans—and loose sweaters or oxford shirts. Ties were a definite no-no. He hated the damn things. Her father had never minded, and evidently, neither did she.

Maggie shut the door behind her and lifted her chin. She was a mere twenty-two years old, yet she managed to imbue her tone with all the seriousness of a wizened sage. "We need to talk."

Eric smiled the smile he reserved just for

Maggie. The one with no teeth showing, just a tiny curling at the corners of his mouth, barely noticeable, while his eyes remained intent and direct. He knew it made her uneasy, which was why he did it, cad that he was. Why should he be the only one suffering? Besides, seeing Maggie squirm was like refined foreplay, and he took undeniable satisfaction in being the one who engineered it. These days she was so set on displaying confidence, on proving herself while fulfilling the role her father had provided, it was a major accomplishment to be the one man who could put a dent in her facade.

He relished the small private games between them, the subtle battle for the upper hand. He wanted the old Maggie back, yet was intrigued by her new persona.

Eric leaned forward, propping his elbows on his desk amid the scattered papers. He did his job as well as ever, and managed to contain his nearly uncontainable lust. There surely wasn't much more she could ask of him. "What is it you think we need to talk about, Maggie?"

Her indrawn breath lifted her delicate breasts beneath the wool jacket. When he'd first met her several years ago, he'd thought her a bit lacking in that department. Then she'd shown up one hot summer day, braless in a college T-shirt, and the air-conditioning had caused her nipples to draw into stiff little points—which had caused various parts of him to stiffen—and since then he'd been mesmerized by her delicacy. He wanted to hold her in his hands, smooth her nipples with his thumbs, then his tongue, tease them with his teeth. . . .

Her jaw firmed and she pushed herself away from the door, catching her hands together at the small of her back and pacing to the front of his desk in a grand confrontation. "I want to talk about your attitude and lack of participation since I've stepped into my father's position."

Eric eyed her rigid stance. She was such a sweet, inexperienced woman that she'd at first misinterpreted his lust for jealousy. She'd assumed, and he supposed with good reason, that he resented her instant leap into the role of president of Carmichael Athletic Supplies. Most men would have. Eric had worked long and hard for Drake Carmichael, and under his guidance, the close personal business had grown. It was still a friendly company with a family atmosphere and very loyal employees, but the presiding stock Maggie inherited had doubled in worth from the year before—thanks to Eric. Because of that, Eric wasn't the only one who had assumed he was next in line for the presidency.

But in truth, Eric didn't give a damn about

his position on the corporate ladder, except that he didn't like the idea of having Maggie for his boss. It put an awkward slant to the things he'd wanted with her, throwing the dynamics of a relationship all out of whack. Maggie wasn't a woman you messed around with; she was the marrying kind. Only now, if he pursued her for his wife, some might assume he was still going after the company in the only way left to him. That not only nettled his pride, it infuriated his sense of possessiveness toward her. He wouldn't let anyone shortchange her worth.

So he'd assured her immediately that he had no desire to be president, no desire to usurp her new command. She'd looked equally stunned by his declaration, and bemused.

Still, he had hoped Maggie might tire of being the boss. She had always seemed like a free spirit to him, a woman meant to pursue her interests in the arts and her joy of traveling. She was a very creative person, fanciful, a daydreamer who had only learned the business to please her father, or so he'd assumed. Eric thought she'd merely been going through the motions when she worked first in the stock room, then briefly on the sales floor, before eventually making her way all the way to the top—at her father's request.

But he had to give her credit; she knew what she was doing. Like all new people, she needed a helping hand now and then in order to familiarize herself with how operations had already been handled, but she was daring enough to try new things and had enough common sense not to rock too many boats at one time. The employees all respected her, and the people they dealt with accepted her command.

He'd do nothing to upset that balance, because contrary to his predictions, she hadn't gotten frazzled and bored with corporate business. She'd dug in with incredible determination and now, within six months of taking over, Maggie had a firm grasp of all aspects of the company.

Eric, in the meantime, suffered the hellish agonies of unrequited lust and growing tenderness.

Shoving his chair back, Eric came to his feet and circled his desk to stand in front of Maggie. This close, he could inhale her scent and feel the nearly electric charge of their combined chemistry. Surely she felt it, too—which probably explained why she'd begun visiting his office more often. Eric got the distinct feeling that Maggie *liked* his predicament.

Tilting his head, he asked, "Why don't you drop the president aura and just talk to me like you used to, Maggie?" Six months ago, when her father had first passed away, Maggie had clung to him while she'd grieved. Eric had settled her in his lap, held her tight, and let her cry until his shirt was soaked. The emotions he'd felt in that moment had nearly brought him to his knees.

Nothing had been right between them since.

Eric crossed his arms over his chest and watched a faint blush color her cheeks.

He loved how Maggie blushed, the soft rose color that tinted her skin and the heat that glowed in her eyes. She blushed over everything—a good joke, a hard laugh, a sly smile. He could only imagine how she'd blush in the throes of a mind-blowing climax, her body damp with sweat from their exertions. . . . *Down, boy.*

"How long," Eric asked, trying to distract himself, "have I known you, honey?"

A small teasing smile flitted across her mouth. "I was seventeen when Daddy hired you."

"So let's see . . . that's five years? Too damn long for you to traipse in here and act so impersonal, wouldn't you say?" If he could only get things back on a strictly friendly basis, maybe, just maybe, he could deal with the powerful physical attraction between them.

"Yes." She sighed, letting out a long breath and clasping her hands together in front of her. "I'm sorry, Eric. It's just . . . well, since taking over, so many people have been watching me, waiting for me to fall on my face. I feel like I'm under constant scrutiny."

"And you think I'm one of those people?"

She met his gaze, then admitted slowly, "I don't know. Despite what you've said, I know you thought—*everyone* thought—that you'd be the president, not me." There was an emotion in her face that seemed almost . . . hopeful. No, that couldn't be.

"I already explained about that, Maggie."

"I know." She gave a long, dramatic sigh. "But you've been so . . . I don't know, *distant,* since I took over."

And she'd been so damn beguiling.

Eric had done his damnedest to come to terms with a radical chink in his plans. He wanted her. Looking at her now with her hair pulled sleekly to one side by a gold clip, her clothes too sophisticated for her spirit, her heels bringing her five-foot-eight-inch height up enough to make her within kissing level to his six-foot-even length . . .

God, but he wanted her. She had her back to the desk and he could have gladly cleared it in an instant, then lowered her gently and parted her long sleek thighs. The thought of exploring her soft female flesh, of coaxing her to a wet readiness, made him shake. He knew without the slightest doubt how well they'd fit together.

He cleared his throat as he thrust his hands

into his pockets and tried to inconspicuously adjust his trousers. "It's the holiday season, hon," he said with a nonchalance he didn't feel. "Lots to do, not only at work, but at home, too. You know that. If you need anything—"

She waved that away. "You've been very helpful here, Eric. I never could have made the transition so smoothly if you hadn't been giving me so much assistance."

That made him frown. "Nonsense. The transition was smooth because you worked hard to make it so. Don't shortchange yourself, Maggie. Drake would have been damn proud if he could see how you've filled his shoes without a hitch."

A short laugh escaped her, even as she began to relax. She stared out the window to the left of his desk. A gentle swirl of snowflakes softened the darkening day. "Daddy's wishes," she said quietly, while sneaking a somewhat shy peek at him, "might not have been as clear as you think."

Eric frowned at those cryptic words, sensing she meant to tell him something, but having no idea what it might be. "You want to explain that, Maggie?"

"No." She shook her head, determination replacing the vulnerability he'd witnessed. "Never mind."

"Maggie . . ." he said, making it sound like a warning.

She sighed again. "There've been plenty of hitches, Eric. Believe me."

A feeling of menace invaded Eric's muscles, making him tense. "Has someone been giving you a hard time?" He stepped closer, willing her to meet his gaze. He'd specifically warned everyone that if they valued their jobs, they'd better work with her, not against her, or he'd personally see them out the door.

"No!" She reached out and touched his biceps in a reassuring gesture. Her touch was at first impersonal, and then gently caressing. God, did she know she was playing with fire?

She drew a shuddering breath. "No, Eric, it's nothing like that. We have the very best employees around."

Eric barely heard her; his rational mind stopped functioning the moment her small hand landed on his arm. She was warm and soft and her scent—that of sweet innocence and spicy sexuality—drifted in to him. He inhaled sharply, and she dropped her hand, tipping her head to study him.

"The problem," she said, now watching him curiously, "is that I've been ultra-popular since taking over."

A new feeling of unease threatened to choke

him. "What the hell does that mean?" He propped his hands on his hips and glared. "Have the guys here been hitting on you?"

"Yes, of course they have." Her simplistic reply felt like the kick of a mule, and then she continued, oblivious to his growing rage. "Not just the guys here, but the men we deal with, men from neighboring businesses, men from—"

"I get the picture!" Eric paced away, then back again. It was bad enough that the female employees had, for some insane reason, decided he was fair game and had been coming on to him in force. But the males were hitting on Maggie, too? Forget the holiday spirit of generosity—he wanted to break some heads!

"You realize," he growled, deciding she could do with a dose of reality, "that it's not your sexy legs and big brown eyes they're after?"

She blinked at him and that intriguing blush warmed her skin. "You think I have sexy legs?"

Eric drew back. Damn, he hadn't meant to say that. Just as he didn't mean to glance down at her legs, and then not be able to look away. Her legs were long and slender and shapely and they went on forever. He'd seen her in jeans, in shorts, in miniskirts. He'd studied those long legs and visualized them around his hips clasping him tight, or better yet, over his shoulders as he clasped her bottom and entered her so deeply. . . .

"Eric?"

He shook his head and croaked, "You have great legs, sweetheart, really. But the point is—"

"And my eyes?"

She watched him, those big dark eyes consuming him, begging for the words. "You have bedroom eyes," he whispered, forgetting his resolve to keep her at a distance. "Big and soft. Inviting."

"Oh."

His voice dropped despite his intentions. "A man could forget himself looking into your eyes."

Her face glowed and she primped. "I had no idea."

Eric locked his jaw against the temptation to show her just how lost he already was. "The point," he said in a near growl, "is that many of the men hitting on you are probably only after the damn company."

"I'm not an idiot. I know that already."

"They think if they . . . What do you mean, you know?"

"That's what I was talking about," she said with a reasonableness Eric had a hard time grasping. "I've been in or around this business for ages—as I already said, since I was seventeen. Most of the men ignored me. I mean, I realize I'm kind of gangly and people saw me as a little too flighty. No," she said when he started to argue with her, appalled by her skewed perceptions of herself. "I'm not fishing for more compliments. I'm a realist, Eric. I know who and what I am. But the point is that men who have always ignored me or only been distantly polite suddenly want to take me to the Bahamas for a private weekend winter getaway, or—"

"*What?*"

"—or they want to give me expensive gifts or—"

"Who the hell asked you to the Bahamas?"

"It doesn't matter, it's just—"

"It most certainly does matter!" Eric felt tense from his toes to his ears. He was forcibly keeping away from her, refusing to involve her in an affair, and equally opposed to making her the object of speculation and office gossip. He'd be damned before he let some other bozo—especially one with dishonorable intentions—cozy up to her. "Who was it, Maggie?"

She touched him again, this time on his chest. "Eric." Like a sigh, she breathed his name, and once again her eyes were huge. "I appreciate your umbrage on my behalf, really I do. But I don't need you to play my white knight."

His tongue stuck to the roof of his mouth. Ridiculous for a thirty-two-year-old man to go mute just because of a simple touch. And on his chest, for God's sake. Not anyplace important. Not where he'd really love for her to touch him.

But he'd wanted her for five long years, and then been denied her just when he'd thought his waiting was about over. He mentally shook himself out of his stupor and framed her face in his hands. Her skin was so warm, so smooth, his heartbeat threatened to break his ribs. "If anyone—and I do mean anyone—insults you in any way, Maggie, I want you to promise to tell me."

Her eyes darkened, and she stared at his mouth. "Okay."

"Your father was one of my best friends." *Good,* he thought, *a tack that makes sense, a reason for my unreasonable reaction.* "Drake would have expected me to help take care of you, to watch out for you."

Just like that, the heat left her eyes. She gave him a withering half smile, patted his left hand, and then pulled it away from her face. Stepping back, she put some space between them and propped her hip on the edge of his desk.

She once again wore her damn professional mien that never failed to set his teeth on edge.

"I appreciate the sentiment, Eric, but I'm a

big girl. I know that even though you don't want the company, others do and they're not above trying to marry me for it. But I can take care of myself."

Goddamn it, *he* wanted to take care of her. But he couldn't very well say so without running the risk of sounding like all the others. If only he hadn't been so noble, if only he'd told her from the beginning how much he wanted her. But she had been so young. . . .

Eric nodded his head, feeling incredibly grim. "Just keep it in mind."

Her smile was a bit distracted. "It's almost time to call it a day, so I'd better get to the point of my visit, huh?"

"All right." Eric watched her as she stood and began edging toward the door.

"The annual Christmas party. I heard from Margo that you don't plan to attend?"

Margo had a big mouth; he'd have to talk to her about that. "I haven't decided yet," he lied, because he had no intention of forcing himself into her company any more than he had to.

"Margo said you turned her down."

Eric rubbed the back of his neck. "Yeah, I didn't . . ."

"I understood that you'd turned everyone down. Margo, Janine, Sally . . ."

"I know who I've spoken with, Maggie. You don't need to remind me." Hell, half the female employees had asked him to the party. He wondered how Maggie knew that, though.

She stared him in the eye. "You, uh, aren't dating anyone right now, are you?"

Eric frowned at her, wondering what she was getting at. It wasn't like her to get involved in his personal life. "No, I'm not dating anyone right now." Despite the female employees' efforts, there was no one he wanted except Maggie, so he'd been suffering a self-assigned celibacy that was about to make him crazed.

"Excellent." She lifted her chin with a facade of bravado and announced boldly, "Then you can go with me. I . . . I need you, Eric."

Chapter 2

Maggie watched as Eric gave her his most intimidating frown. Good Lord, the man was gorgeous. Her father had accused her of an infatuation, calling her obsession with his right-hand man *puppy love*. Granted, at seventeen, it could have been nothing else. But she was twenty-two now, and there was nothing immature or flighty about her feelings for Eric Bragg.

She was getting downright desperate to get his attention, and her New Year's resolution, made a bit early out of necessity, was to seduce him. It would be a Christmas present to herself. At least an office fling would give her something, if not what she really wanted. And perhaps, with any luck, once she'd made love to him he'd begin to see her as a woman, rather than the boss's daughter.

Eric looked dazed. His broad shoulders were tensed and his legs were braced apart as if he had to struggle for his balance. Hazel eyes narrowed, he rasped, "Come again?"

Being cowardly, Maggie inched a tiny bit closer to the door and escape, should Eric's response prove too humiliating to bear. Admittedly, she lacked experience. But she felt certain that he'd been giving her mixed signals. Sometimes he patted her head like she was still seventeen, and then every so often he'd throw her for a loop, like his comment on her legs, accompanied by a certain hot look in his eyes. . . .

"I need you," she blurted again. It was easier saying it the second time, but not much. "I want to attend the party. As the boss, I'm pretty much obligated to go. But so many of the male employees and associates have asked me, and I wasn't sure how to refuse them without causing a personal rift—so I lied and said I already had a date. You."

"Me?"

Nodding, she added, "It's just for pretend. I mean, you won't be expected to spend any money on me or dote on me or anything. But I might as well come clean and tell you that everyone also assumes you're helping me organize the Christmas party."

"Maggie . . ."

He sounded choked and she didn't know if it was anger or not. If he was mad, she'd have to scrap the second step of this evening's plan. That is, if her lack of courage didn't cause her to scrap it anyway. She reached behind her and felt for the doorknob. "Don't worry about it. I've got everything under control, so you don't have to really do much for the party. Except make others think you're helping me." Which she hoped would force them into some isolated time together. She bit her lip with the thought. "I'll give you a . . ."—she had to clear her throat—"Christmas bonus for helping out."

"I don't want a goddamned Christmas bonus from you," he growled, and started toward her with a dark frown.

Maggie felt her mouth drop open when he stopped a mere inch in front of her. Her entire body was zinging with awareness, the way it always did whenever Eric was close. His hazel eyes were intent and probing and they made her feel like he could see right into her soul.

She'd often wondered if he looked at a woman like that while making love to her.

She swallowed audibly with the visual images filling her brain.

"You're mad?" She wanted it clarified before she went any further.

"With your assumption that you need to reward me for helping. You're damn right."

"Oh." Well, that was good, wasn't it? Definitely. "Okay, so you *will* help?"

He gave an aggrieved sigh. "Yes."

So far, so good. "Will you also accompany me to the party?"

Flattening one hand on the door, Eric leaned toward her. Despite his dark frown, there was something else in his eyes, something expectant. He looked at her mouth, and his jaw clenched. "Yes."

She licked her lips, saw his eyes narrow, and shivered. "The thing is," she said, sounding a bit breathless, "I have to give you a bonus. I'm giving everyone a bonus, so if I don't, the employees might begin to talk."

He stilled, then leaned away from her again, shoving his hands deep into his pants pockets. He scowled. "That would bother you? If they talked, I mean?"

She didn't want anyone to say anything negative about Eric! Her possessiveness over him had amused her father, but he'd promised never to say a thing to Eric, and as far as she knew, he hadn't.

What her father had done instead was worse, because it had backfired in a big way. "I just think we should avoid gossip whenever possible."

Looking resigned, Eric nodded. "What do you want me to do for the party? Hell, I don't even know what goes into planning a party. I've never done it before."

Maggie tried a nervous smile. "As I said, most of it is taken care of. But I had those offers from the guys . . . so I said you were helping. That's okay?"

He gave a sharp nod, distracted by some inner thought.

"The hall and caterers are taken care of. And I've already started to . . . well, decorate the offices a little."

Some of the rigidness left Eric's shoulders. She loved his body, how hard it was, how tall and strong. He did nothing to emphasize his muscular bulk, but his leisurely attempts at style managed it anyway. He always rolled his shirtsleeves up to his elbows, displaying his thick wrists and solid forearms. Even the look of his watch on his wrist, surrounded by dark crisp hair, seemed incredibly sensual and masculine. And his open shirt collar, which showed even more hair on his chest, made her feel too warm in too many places. She imagined he was somewhat hairy all over, but she wanted to know for sure. She wanted to touch him everywhere.

His walk was long and easy, his strength something he took for granted. His corduroy slacks appeared soft and were sometimes worn shiny in the most delectable places—like across his fly.

She forced herself to quit staring and met his gaze. "Why are you smiling?"

"Because I like seeing you enthused about something again."

Her eyes nearly crossed in her embarrassment. He knew how enthusiastic she was about his body?

Eric chuckled at her startled expression. "I remember how excited you used to get over Christmas." He reached out and touched her gold barrette with one long, rough finger. "What happened to those cute little bells you used to wear, Maggie?"

Cute? She'd assumed that she was far too immature for Eric, what with her silly holiday dressing. So she'd tried to look more sophisticated, more mature, in order to get his attention. But every day it had seemed like additional distance had come between them.

Her father had thought the lure of the company would be enough to get Eric to notice her. The letter he'd included to her in his will had stated as much. He was giving her a chance at the man she wanted, and she loved him so much for his well-meaning efforts. But instead of having the desired result, Eric wanted less to do with her than ever.

He'd said he didn't want the presidency. Evidently he didn't want her, either. Yet. But she was working on it.

Maggie pulled the door open and prayed he wouldn't notice the mistletoe until it was too late. "I'm not eighteen anymore, Eric. And I'm the boss. I can't be caught dashing up and down the hallways, jingling with bells and disturbing everyone."

He stepped into the doorframe with her. "You never disturbed me, hon." His eyes darkened and his mouth tilted in a crooked, thoroughly endearing smile. "At least, not the way you think."

Maggie had no idea what he meant by that, and besides, she needed all her concentration to screw up her daring. She drew a deep breath, smiled, and then said, "Oh, look. We're under the mistletoe."

Eric faltered for just a heartbeat, but she moved too quickly for him. Grabbing his neck with both hands, she pulled him down as she went on tiptoe. She heard his indrawn breath, felt the heat of his big body, and then her mouth was smashed over his and lights exploded behind her eyelids.

She moaned.

Eric held very still. "Uh, Maggie?" he whispered against her lips.

"Hmmm?" No way was she letting him go yet. This was very, very nice.

She felt the touch of his right hand in her hair, then his left was at her waist and he said in a low, rough rumble, "If we're going to do this, baby, let's do it right."

Maggie's eyes opened in surprise, but slowly sank shut again as Eric drew her so close that their bodies blended together from hips to shoulders. Her breasts, feeling remarkably sensitive, flattened against the hard wall of his chest. Her pelvis cradled his, and she became aware of his erection, which literally stole her breath away.

He wanted her? He liked kissing her?

His large hand opened on the small of her back and urged her closer still, until she felt his every pulsing heartbeat in the most erotic way possible. With a subtle shifting of his head, his mouth settled more comfortably against hers and he took control of the kiss. And wow, what a kiss it was!

He left her mouth for a brief moment to nuzzle beneath her ear. "Relax, Maggie."

What a ludicrous suggestion! She felt strung so tight, her body throbbed. "Okay."

She gave him all her weight and sighed as every pleasurable sensation intensified. His open mouth left a damp trail from her throat to her chin to her lips. She shivered. His tongue slid over her lips, teasing, and then into her mouth. *Oh, God.* She tried to stay calm, but it was so incredible, so delicious, that her breath came faster and her nipples tingled into hard tips and a sweet ache expanded low in her belly.

Eric growled low, a primitive response that thrilled her. His tongue, damp and hot, stroked deeply into her, over her own tongue, tasting her, exploring her.

Her hands knotted in his shirt, she arched into him, and then—she heard the tiny twitter of a feminine laugh.

Stunned when Eric suddenly pulled away, Maggie would have stumbled if he hadn't kept her upright with one strong arm wrapped around her waist. He glared over his shoulder, and there stood his secretary and two male employees.

Mortified heat exploded beneath Maggie's

skin, making her dizzy. Everyone stood in heavy silence.

She was the boss, Maggie told herself, she had to take control of this small turn in events. Clearing her throat even as she stepped out of Eric's reach, Maggie said, "Well. I thought everyone had gone home already." She raised a brow, silently asking for an explanation.

"We were just about to leave," his secretary, Janine, informed them.

Eric dropped back to lean against the doorframe and crossed his arms over his chest. He seemed either oblivious or unconcerned with the fact that he had a very noticeable erection. Despite the impropriety, it thrilled Maggie, because at least that meant he was interested.

Of course, she had been rubbing up against him rather thoroughly, and that could account for the physical reaction. Mere friction?

Maggie stepped in front of him, shielding him with her body, and pointed up. "Mistletoe," she explained to her audience.

The secretary smiled like a damned cat and glided forward, her intent plain. "So I see. How . . . fortunate."

Not about to let anyone else touch Eric now that she'd gotten him revved up, Maggie stationed herself in front of him like a sentinel. When the secretary merely looked at her, Maggie made a shooing motion with her hands.

"Go on home, Janine. I'm not approving any overtime today. Go on."

Janine barely bit back a smile. "But . . ."

Eric, sounding on the verge of laughter, said, "I think it's just the mistletoe she's after, Maggie, not more pay."

Maggie sent him a quelling glance over her shoulder, before addressing the woman again. "There's more down the hall," Maggie assured her, trying to shoo her on her way. "I put some in all the doorways. You two," she added, pointing to the men, both of whom had been pursuing her earlier, "go with her. Find some mistletoe. Go."

The men, displaying a sense of discretion, hid their amusement and escorted the willing secretary out. Maggie glared at them until they were completely gone from sight, mumbling under her breath about pushy women.

"You want to explain that?" Eric asked.

"Hmmm?" Maggie turned to face him. "Explain what?"

"Why you turned into a ferocious amazon just because Janine wanted to kiss me. I mean, kissing is the purpose of mistletoe, right? And you're the one who hung it in my doorway."

"Well." Of course kissing was the point, but she wanted to be the only one taking advantage of it with Eric.

Maggie couldn't quite look at him as she

tried to figure out how to get things back on track. Which meant getting his mouth back on hers, his hands touching her again. "I put you in that awkward situation by kissing you," she muttered, thinking it out as she went along, "so I didn't want you to feel . . . obligated . . . to kiss anyone else. I was . . . protecting you."

"So you don't personally care if Janine kisses me? I mean, if the mistletoe stays there, I assume she'll take care of it in the morning."

It was hard to speak with her teeth clenched. "No," she ground out, nearly choking on the lie. "If you want to kiss Janine, that's certainly your business."

His eyes narrowed. "I see." In the next instant he surprised her by plucking the mistletoe down and shoving it into his pants pocket.

Maggie gave a silent prayer of relief. But when she peeked up at him, she felt doubly foolish for the confusion and annoyance on his face.

"I don't want to kiss Janine," he explained.

"Good." *Get it moving, Maggie.* "I mean, then since that's settled, perhaps . . ."

"Maggie?" When she pretended a great need to straighten her jacket, Eric reached out and tilted up her chin. "Why did you kiss me, sweetheart?"

She gulped. He wanted explanations? Good grief, she hadn't expected that. She'd planned on carrying things through should he prove agreeable, or slinking away if he rebuffed her. But not once had she considered an interrogation, for crying out loud.

Men, in her limited experience, were either interested or not, but they never wanted to talk about it!

"I . . . ah, I was trying to get you into the Christmas spirit."

Eric released her and frowned thoughtfully. "You're embarrassed?" She denied that with a shake of her head, so he pointed out, "Your face is red."

She was horny. Turned on. Aroused. All hot and bothered. "I'm not embarrassed."

He quirked one brow.

"It was just a simple kiss, after all." And at twenty-two, she'd had as many kisses as any other woman her age. *But none like that. None with Eric.* Oh, it was different, all right, just as different as she'd always known it would be. "We've both been kissed plenty, right? No big deal."

His frown turned fierce, and she figured she'd managed to tick him off after all. "All right, then." She clasped her hands together and gave him a beatific smile. "Since you agreed to help me with the Christmas party, I guess we're all settled."

She started away, bent only on retreat before

she blew it completely, but Eric's voice stopped her. "When do we start, Maggie?"

She hesitated. "Uh . . . how about tomorrow? At my place? That is, if you don't already have a date for the weekend. . . ."

"I'll be there at two o'clock."

Two? In the afternoon? She'd really been hoping for something toward the evening, when she'd be able to light some candles, put a fire in the fireplace, set the mood for seduction. . . .

She realized Eric was waiting, staring at her in speculation, and she smiled as if she had not a care in the world. If he got suspicious, if he guessed at everything she wanted to do to him, he might not come at all. "Two is just fine. I'll see you then."

Eric managed to wait all of five minutes before curiosity got the better of him and he made his way to Maggie's office. If he'd read her right—and he was fairly certain he had—she wanted him. Not as much as he wanted her: that was impossible. But while he'd made a resolution not to seduce her, he hadn't figured on her trying to seduce him!

Despite everything he'd told himself about how disastrous a relationship would be, he knew damn good and well he wouldn't be able to resist her now that she'd shown some interest. She was lucky he'd let her walk away at all, much less promised to wait until two the next day. If he'd been thinking clearly, he'd have pulled her back into his office, locked the door, and made use of the desk as he'd envisioned earlier.

He told himself it didn't matter that all they could have was an affair. Maggie had already made it clear what she thought about someone chasing her for the company. If he tried to take things beyond an affair, she'd forever wonder what he'd really wanted. And then, too, there'd be the jokes about him trying to screw his way to the top. The idea was intolerable. Especially since she didn't want any gossip. Marrying the boss, which was what he really wanted to do, would certainly stir up the speculation.

Damn, he didn't have many choices.

When Eric opened her office door, he knew right away that she was already gone. All the lights were out and, as usual, her desk was neatly cleared of all the day's work. Maggie was tidy to a fault.

Then he noticed a paper on the floor.

Evidently she'd been as rattled as he after that killer kiss. Perhaps she'd left in a hurry, anxious to get home to the same cold shower he now anticipated. Although actually, looking out the window toward the frozen winter landscape, he realized that just getting to his car was liable to cool down his lust.

Knowing he was condemned to a lonely night of erotic frustration made Eric want to howl. Unlike Maggie, he wasn't in a hurry to head home, where the solitude would cause him to dwell on all the sensual things he wanted to do to Maggie Carmichael, and all the explicit things he wanted her to do to him.

But the cleaning crew, who came by every Friday evening, would be arriving soon. He had no choice but to be on his way. He stepped forward to retrieve the piece of paper in case it was anything important, meaning to simply place it on her desk.

One typed word, about midway through the text, seemed to leap right out at him. *Thrust*. He leaned against the edge of her desk and read the sentence: *She was hot and wet and his fingers thrust into her easily, eliciting a cry from deep in her throat*. Eric nearly dropped the paper.

He locked his knees as his pulse quickened and his body reacted to that one simple sentence. Quickly, his gaze flicked up to the header on the paper and he read: *Magdelain Yvonne, Heated Storm, pg. 81.* Magdelain Yvonne? That was Maggie! Magdelain Yvonne Carmichael.

Maggie had written this?

Numb, moving by rote, Eric pulled out her desk chair and sank into it, his eyes still glued to the paper in his hand. A small lighted ceramic Christmas tree, situated at the corner of her desk, provided all the illumination he needed. He started at the top of the page and began reading.

It was by far the most sensual, erotic, explicit passage he'd ever read outside of porn. But porn was unemotional and there was nothing unemotional in the deeply provocative love scene his Maggie had written.

When the paper ended—right in the middle of the female protagonist experiencing a gut-wrenching orgasm thanks to the guy's patience and talented fingers—Eric nearly groaned. His own hand clenched into a fist as he considered touching Maggie in just that way, watching her face while he made her come, feeling her body tighten around his fingers, feeling her wetness, her heat, and hearing her hoarse cry.

Where the hell was the rest of it?

Frantically he looked at her desk, moving papers aside and lifting files, but it was all business-related things. He opened a drawer and peeked inside, feeling like a total bounder but unable to stop himself. The drawer had only more files and notations in it. So he tried the others. Finally, in the drawer at the bottom of her desk, hidden beneath a thick thesaurus, he found the rest of the manuscript.

With no hesitation at all he slipped page 81

into place and settled back in the chair to read from the beginning. He was still there when the cleaning crew arrived. He'd just reached the end—which wasn't the end at all. Maggie needed several more chapters to finish the story, but already Eric could tell that she was very talented. He'd gotten so absorbed in the story he'd almost forgotten it was written by Maggie, and simply began enjoying it.

When he had remembered it was written by Maggie, he'd been hit with such a wave of lust he broke out in a sweat.

He'd never read a romance. He'd had no idea they were so good, so full of fast-paced plot and great characterization. Just like his mystery novels, only with more emphasis on the emotional side of the relationship. And lots more sex. *Great sex.* He liked it.

The only problem, to his mind, was the physical descriptions of the characters. The blond female was voluptuous, with large breasts and generously rounded hips and a brazenness that Eric had to admit was sexy as sin. She in no way resembled Maggie.

So why the hell did the male character so closely resemble him?

Maggie had given him the same height, same eyes, same dark hair. Even some of the things the guy said were words right out of Eric's mouth. And his wardrobe . . . well, he had the exact same clothes hanging in his closet at home.

The only major difference was that the guy in the story had finally gotten the heroine naked and in the sack for some really hot action. Hell, not only that, but he'd come three times thanks to the heroine's enthusiasm, something Eric wasn't even sure was possible.

Yet Eric was going home each night to an empty bed.

Well beyond the crazed stage, Eric was highly affronted, and jealous, that his fictitious character could take what he'd denied himself.

Was this, perhaps, what Maggie really wanted?

His heart pounded with both excitement and resentment. Ha! He was on to her now. It made his insides clench to realize she wasn't nearly as inexperienced as he'd always let himself believe. No way could she have devised such graphic sex scenes out of the depth of imagination.

In hindsight, he admitted Maggie was too sexy, too vivacious, to have stayed inexperienced for long. His nobility in attempting to wait had come back and bitten him in the ass. But that was over with now. She wanted him, had made love to him in fiction, and no more would he play the gallant schmuck, giving her plenty of time and space.

If Maggie wanted to write about sexual satisfaction, he'd show her sexual satisfaction! She'd started this tonight with her damned mistletoe and her teasing and her invitations.

His little Maggie was in for a hell of a surprise.

Despite Eric's heated plans, it bothered him immensely to put the book back in her drawer, where anyone might be able to find it. He'd have to talk to her about that—after he showed her that no fictitious character had anything on him when it came to reality.

He buried the manuscript under books and papers, just as she'd had it, then piled in a few more things, trying to be extra cautious. He was aware of a fine tension in his muscles, a touch of aroused excitement.

Eric glanced at his watch, saw that it was seven o'clock, and by the time he could reach Maggie's, it'd likely be eight. But that wasn't so late, and now he had a damn good reason to call on her tonight. He felt for the mistletoe he'd put in his pocket, and grinned when his fingers closed around it.

Maggie was a writer. A very talented, very erotic writer. And she wanted him; he had no more doubts about that. If he couldn't have

Maggie for a wife, at least he could have this, and if all went as planned, she'd be his, not in matrimony, but in a basic, physical way that was even more binding.

For the first time in six months, things seemed to be getting back on track.

Chapter 3

Maggie hurried out of the shower when she heard the doorbell peal. The pizza she'd ordered must have arrived early, so she trotted out of the room even as she pulled on her oldest, thickest robe. Her wet hair was wrapped in a towel, turban-style, and her bare feet left damp indentations in the plush carpet.

On the way to the door she made certain her

cloth belt was securely tied and grabbed money for a tip. She ordered so many pizzas that the owner of the small restaurant let her run a tab, which she paid at the end of each month.

She wrenched the door open just as the doorbell chimed again. "Sorry, you got here quicker than . . . I . . . thought. . . ."

Eric stood there, snowflakes clinging to his midnight hair, his cheeks ruddy from the cold, his gaze blazing with some emotion that she couldn't begin to decipher. At the sight of her, his eyes narrowed and did a slow study of her from head to toe. She felt it like a tactile stroke, flesh on flesh. Ignoring her mute surprise, he stepped in, which forced her to step back. Holding her gaze, he pushed the door shut.

Maggie shivered. A cold blast of winter air had preceded Eric, but that wasn't what caused the gooseflesh to rise on her damp skin. No, Eric brought with him the scent of the brisk outdoors, his delicious cologne, and his own unique smell, guaranteed to make her melt. She never failed to react to it with a delicate shudder and a hungry tingling inside.

He looked so good, and here she stood looking her worst! Her makeup was gone, her hair in a towel, and her robe was so ratty it would have been generous to describe it as broken-in.

"You expecting someone?"

There was a growled undertone to his words that Maggie didn't understand. She pressed her hands to her warm cheeks even as she began to explain. "I thought you were the pizza guy."

The frown disappeared. With a small predatory smile, Eric looked her over once again, and there was so much heat, so much satisfaction in his gaze, she suddenly felt too warm for the thick robe. "Do you always greet deliverymen dressed like this?"

"No." She pulled the lapels of her robe together at her throat, a five-dollar bill clenched in her fist. "I thought he was early. Usually I have plenty of time to shower and change. I could have just let him leave the pizza outside the door, but I wanted to tip him. It is almost Christmas, and the weather isn't the best. . . ."

Eric reached out and slowly plucked the money from her hand. In the process his knuckles grazed lightly over the top of her breast, across her chest and throat. "Sweetheart, if you answer the door that way, you won't need any further tip, believe me."

Mouth hanging open, she blinked at him, dazed by what she assumed—*hoped*—was a compliment. Eric gazed briefly at her mouth before abruptly turning away. Maggie watched as he laid the money on the entry table and then looked around her home with frank interest. She cleared her throat. "I . . . I didn't expect you tonight."

"I know." He said the words gently, and with some great, hidden meaning. "I changed my mind about waiting until tomorrow. Am I interrupting any plans?"

None that she would mind having interrupted. She'd hoped to work on her book for a few hours, which was why she'd ordered the fast food. Whenever she typed, she ate. The two just seemed to go hand in hand, which, because she was always pressed for time since taking over for her father, was a blessing. Heaven knew she rarely had time for a sit-down meal. "I was just going to get some . . . work done."

"Ah." He gave her a wicked, suggestive grin. "Maybe I can help?"

She got warm with just the thought. Eric help her with her writing? She didn't think so. For now, she was still a closet writer, not telling any of her nonwriting friends. As the president of the company, she couldn't imagine how her business associates might react to the fact she wrote very racy romance novels. She wasn't ashamed of what she did, but she simply didn't need the added hassle of speculation. At various conventions, she'd heard all the jeers and jokes about how a romance writer researched. For her, research on the love scenes was simply daydreaming about Eric. There were parts of him in every hero she created; there had to be, for her to consider the men heroes.

Until she resolved the issue of her new position in the company, she wouldn't breathe a word about her need to create characters and romances.

"It's nothing that can't wait." Belatedly, she realized they were still standing just inside the door. She blushed again. "Come on in."

His hand lifted to trail along a looping pine garland, fastened in place around her doorframe with bright red and silver bows. He seemed intrigued by her Christmas decorations, examining the dancing Santa on the table where he'd placed her five-dollar tip, before gazing across the room to her collections of candles displayed on the fireplace mantel and the corner of the counter that separated her kitchen from her living space.

Every tabletop held some sort of Christmas paraphernalia, old and new. Eric was right that she loved the holidays and rejoiced in celebrating them.

Her small, freshly cut tree, heavily laden with ornaments and tinsel and lights, blinked brightly at the opposite side of the room. It fit perfectly in the small nook just in front of her desk and work space.

Eric nodded in satisfaction. "This is more like you."

She raised a brow, questioning.

"The holiday spirit," he explained, but his voice trailed off as his gaze lit on her laptop computer and the piles of paper littering her scarred antique oak desk.

Good grief, she'd all but forgotten about her newest chapters sitting out! From this distance, there was no way Eric could tell what it was, but that didn't reassure her overly. Trying to look nonchalant, Maggie crossed the room and closed her laptop quickly, then stacked the papers and shoved them in a drawer.

Eric watched her so closely, she flinched. "Bringing work home?" he asked.

As he spoke, he pulled off his shearling jacket and hung it on her coat tree beside her wool cape. And just that, the sight of the two garments hanging side by side, made her wistful. It would be so nice if he hung his coat there every night.

"Uh, nothing important." She preferred working on the computer at her office during her lunch breaks, since the monitor was much bigger and easier to see than the laptop. But she also worked at home whenever she could. Finishing up a book on deadline while working a fifty-hour-a-week job was grueling. Once she finished this book, she planned to buy a new computer for her home. But the idea of getting things set up and functioning at this particular moment, with the rush of the holidays, the pressure of a deadline, and her escalating sexual frustration, was more than she could bear. The past six months had been adjustment enough. She didn't need the aggravation of breaking in a new computer.

Eric started toward her with a slow, deliberate stride.

She cleared her throat, gave one last glance at her desk to make sure nothing obvious was still out, then said, "Why don't I get us something to drink?"

She hoped to escape to the kitchen, thinking to divert Eric from his path. Though everything was now put away, she'd feel better if he kept plenty of distance between himself and the desk.

Before she could take two steps, Eric stopped her with a large hand on her elbow. Her living room was small and cozy, but how he'd moved across it so quickly, she couldn't imagine.

"Your place is nice. I haven't seen it before."

Until her father's death, she'd lived in their family home with him. Eric had been to that house many times. But since then, he'd been avoiding her for the most part, despite her efforts to get closer to him.

"After Daddy died," she whispered, "I couldn't quite take living in the house. It seemed too big, too cold, and I missed him too much. So I moved here." Her home was now a moderately sized condominium that suited her perfectly. She had her own small yard, complete with patio and privacy fence, a fireplace, and a balcony off her bedroom.

The space where her desk and various office equipment sat had been intended as a breakfast nook, but she'd commandeered the space for her office.

Her bedroom, a spare room, and the bath were all upstairs. Eric was looking at the heavy desk and she said quickly, "I kept Daddy's desk from home, and some of his furniture."

Maggie watched as Eric made note of the two straight-backed armchairs flanking the fireplace. They were antique also, repadded with a soft velvety material that complemented the subtle striping in her own overstuffed beige, rose, and burgundy sofa. Marble-topped tables that had been in her family for over fifty years were situated at either end of the sofa and each held an array of framed photos and Christmas bric-a-brac. On the matching coffee table was a large glass dish filled with candies, and two more fat candles. Over the warmly glowing parquet floor was a large thick area rug that had once decorated her father's library.

Nodding, his hand still cupped securely

around her arm, Eric said, "You and your father were very close, weren't you?"

The warmth of his hand made casual conversation difficult. "I think more so than most daughters and fathers, because my mother passed away when I was so young." She shrugged, but the sadness never failed to touch her when she thought of her father. "It was always just Dad and me, and he was the best father in the world."

Eric tugged her closer and stood looking down into her face. Memories flitted through her mind, the way he'd held her on his lap and let her cry the day her father had passed away. Eric had been the only other person she'd wanted to grieve with. When she'd come to him, he hadn't questioned her, hadn't hesitated. He'd held her, and she'd been comforted.

Eric lifted his free hand and smoothed her cheek. The touch was intimate and exciting. "I'm sorry you've caught me looking so wretched," she blurted.

He smiled and his hand slipped around her neck, his rough fingertips teasing her skin even as he bent his head. "You look adorable."

Maggie barely absorbed the absurd compliment before the feel of his mouth on hers scattered her wits. But this kiss was gentle and fleeting, his warm mouth there and then gone, leaving her lips tingling, her breath catching. Making her want so much more. She leaned toward him, hoping he'd take the hint—and her doorbell rang.

"You go get dried off," he whispered as he teased the corner of her mouth with his thumb, "and I'll get the pizza."

Flustered, she stepped back and retightened her belt. "It'll just take me a few minutes to change and get my hair combed out."

Eric straightened her chenille lapels, letting the backs of his hands glide over her upper chest, then lower. His knuckles barely fell short of actually coming into contact with her nipples. She gasped, waiting, in an agony of anticipation.

He met her encouraging gaze and ordered in a low voice, "No, don't change. I like this. It's sexy."

"It is?" She looked down at the faded peach robe, threadbare in some spots where the chenille had fallen out from too many washings. Bemusement shook her out of her stupor. "*This* is sexy?"

"Are you naked beneath it?"

She gulped. "Yes."

His hazel eyes glowed with heat. "Damn right it's sexy."

She turned on her heel and stumbled out of the room. Eric appeared to be here for a reason, and her heart was racing so fast she could barely breathe. "I'll be right back," she called over her shoulder.

"Take your time," he answered on his way to her front door, but within five minutes she had her hair combed out and nearly dry, a touch of subtle makeup on, and her best perfume dabbed into the most secret places.

Eric didn't stand a chance.

Eric had set the pizza in the kitchen and was studying Maggie's colorful tree when he felt her presence behind him. He turned slowly and was met with the sight of her bright, expectant gaze. She watched him so closely, he felt singed. Anticipation rode him hard.

Maggie might enjoy writing hot love scenes, but he intended to see that she enjoyed experiencing them even more.

The idea of getting Maggie Carmichael hot made blood surge to his groin, swelling his sex painfully and making his heart race. He wanted everything from her, but he'd take what he could get.

"Come here," he whispered.

Lips parted, her pulse visibly racing, Maggie padded toward him on bare feet. She moved slowly, as if uncertain of his intent. Good. She had teased him at work, tempting him with that killer kiss beneath the mistletoe and then darting away. Did she sense her teasing had come to an end?

When she got close enough, Eric casually looped his arms around her waist. His hands rested on the very top of her sweetly rounded behind. Though his fingers twitched with the need to cuddle her bottom, to see if it was as soft and resilient as he'd always imagined, he didn't give in to the urge. That would be too easy, for both of them.

Nuzzling her cheek, he asked, "Do you know why I'm here, sweetheart?"

Her small palms opened on his chest and she nodded. "I think so."

He lightly bit her neck, making her gasp, then laved the small spot with his tongue. Fresh from her bath, her skin tasted warm and soft and was scented by something other than Maggie herself. That disappointed him. Why did women always try to conceal their own delicious smell with artificial scents?

"You're wearing perfume," he noted out loud.

"I . . . yes."

"Where all did you put it, Maggie?"

Maggie's breath deepened, came faster. She shook her head, as if she didn't understand.

"When I'm this close to you," he said softly, "I want to smell *you.*"

Eric let his hand glide up her waist to the outer curves of her breast. "When I kiss you here," he said, holding her gaze as his thumb brushed inward, just touching the edge of a tightly beaded nipple, "I don't want to be distracted with the smell of perfume. Do you understand?"

Her whole body trembled with her repressed excitement. "Yes."

"And," he added, trailing his fingers slowly downward, watching her, judging her response, "when I kiss you . . . here—"

"Oh, God." Her eyes drifted shut and she shivered.

"I want to know your scent." His fingers brushed, so very gently, between her thighs. Her lips parted, her head tilted back. The robe was thick enough that his touch would only be teasing, but still she jerked.

Eric took the offering of her throat and drew her tender flesh against his teeth, deliberately giving her a hickey. He wanted to mark her as his own—all over. She moaned and snuggled closer to him.

"Damn, you taste good." He waited a heartbeat, letting that sink in, then added in a whisper, "I can't wait to taste you everywhere." His fingers were still between her thighs, cupping her mound, and he pressed warmly against her to let her know exactly what he meant.

Her hands curled into fists, knotting in his shirt. He waited for her to get a visual image of that, already planning his next move while he had her off balance.

Her eyes opened, hotly intent. "I'd like to taste you, too," she answered, and Eric barely bit back his groan.

"Damn." If she got him visualizing things like her mouth on him, he'd never last! He gave a half laugh at her daring, which earned him a startled expression. Maggie never failed to amaze him. "I want this to last, you little tease. Don't push me."

She didn't deny the teasing part, and simply asked, "This?"

"Mmmm." He slipped his hand under her collar and rubbed her nape, feeling the cool slide of her damp, heavy hair over the back of his hand. "I want you so much I'm about to go crazy with it."

"Eric." She breathed his name, attempting to wiggle closer to him.

He held her off. "No, not yet. I need you to want me as much, Maggie."

With her hands clenched in his shirt, she attempted to shake him. He didn't budge, and her brown eyes grew huge and uncertain. "But I do!"

"Shhh." He pressed his thumb over her lips, silencing her. "Not yet. But you will. Soon."

Wind whistled outside the French doors behind her desk, blowing powdery snowflakes against the glass. The twinkle lights on her tree gave a magical glow to the room. Eric stepped away from her, amazed at how difficult it was to do. "You need to eat your pizza before it gets cold."

Maggie's breathing was audible in the otherwise silent room. With a quick glance, Eric saw that her hands were folded over her middle, as if to hold in the sweet ache of desire, and her nipples were thrusting points against the softness of her robe. His testicles tightened, his cock throbbing at this evidence of her arousal, but he refused to make this so easy. He'd been suffering for a hell of a long time, wanting her, yet not wanting to make her unhappy. Now he knew that she was as physically attracted as he. But if that was all they could have, he wanted it to be the best it could be. And that meant being patient.

"Forget the pizza," she said. "I'm . . . I'm not hungry anymore."

Eric noted her stiff posture, the color in her cheeks. "Is that right?"

She lifted her chin in that familiar way that made his heart swell. "I'm hungry for *you*. So stop teasing me."

Against his will, Eric felt his mouth curling in a pleased smile. Maggie liked giving orders, further evidence that she fit the role of "boss" to perfection. He nodded slowly, keeping his gaze locked to her own, and said, "All right, sweetheart."

She accepted his hand when he reached out to her, her slender chilled fingers nestling into his warm palm. Eric turned them toward the sitting area and led Maggie to a single straight-backed chair. The Christmas tree with its soft glow was behind her, lending the only illumination other than the faint light from the kitchen.

Maggie looked at the chair, then at the very soft, long couch, but he could tell she wasn't brazen enough to insist they sit side by side, which he'd been counting on. If they settled together on the couch, she'd end up beneath him in no time and all his seduction would be over before it had really started.

That wouldn't do.

With a soft grumble, more to herself, though he heard her plain enough, Maggie slid into the chair and then fussed with her robe, making certain it folded modestly over her legs. A futile effort on her part, but for the moment he let it go.

Hiding his grin, Eric walked behind Maggie. She stiffened, alert to his every move. Eric touched her hair.

"Do you have any idea how much I loved your hair long?"

Tipping her head back, she looked at him upside down. "No."

Eric smoothed his hands over her throat, and when her lips parted, he leaned down and kissed her lightly. "I used to imagine your hair all spread out on the pillow, *my* pillow."

"But . . ." She started to twist around to face him more surely, and he held her shoulders to still her movements.

"I used to think about the fact that your hair was long enough and thick enough to hide your breasts. You could have stood topless in front of me, and I wouldn't have been able to see a thing. But now"—he slid his hands over her shoulders and cupped her small firm breasts completely—"there's no way you can hide from me. Can you, sweetheart?"

Her back flattened hard against the chair and she held herself rigid, not in fear or rejection, but in surprise. The erratic drumming of her heart teased his palm. God, she felt good. Soft, round. Moving lazily, he chafed her nipples with his open hands until she gripped the arms of the chair in a death hold and her every breath sounded like a stifled moan.

Impatient, Eric loosened the top of her robe and parted it enough to see her pale breasts and her taut pink nipples. He caught his breath.

Just that quickly she jerked away and turned to face him, yanking her robe closed in the process. There was so much vulnerability in her face, he felt his heart softening even as his erection pushed painfully against his slacks.

Her bottom lip quivered and she stilled it by holding it in her teeth. Both hands secured her robe, layering it over her throat so that not a single patch of her soft flesh showed.

Eric slowly circled the chair, never releasing her from his gaze. When he was directly in front of her, her face, as well as her fascinated and wary gaze, on a level with his lap, he laid one large hand on top of her head. Her hair was cool in contrast to the heat he saw in her cheeks. "What is it, babe?"

She squeezed her eyes closed.

"Maggie?" Using one finger, he tipped up her chin. Was he moving too fast, despite her bravado of wanting him to get on with it? He frowned slightly with the thought. "I am going to look at you, you know."

She winced. "It's just that . . . I'm actually sort of . . . small."

Ah. Biting back his smile, Eric knelt in front of her and covered her hands with his own. Carefully wresting them away from their secure hold on fabric and modesty, he said, "You're actually sort of perfect."

She trembled, but met his gaze. "You like big-breasted women."

He remembered the woman in her story, with her full-blown, overripe figure. Was this why she'd put that particular female with his fictional counterpart? He ran his thumb over her knuckles, soothing her, then loosely clasped the lapels of her robe. "What makes you think so?"

She held herself in uncertain anxiety. Did she expect him to rip the robe away despite her wishes? Never would he deliberately push her or make her uneasy. He cared far too much about her for that. No, his plans were for sensual suspense, not embarrassment.

A small sound of frustration, or maybe more like resignation, escaped her. "*All* men like big breasts."

Perched on the edge of her seat, she looked ready to take flight regardless of the fact that Eric was on his knees in front of her, blocking her in. To prevent her from trying to do just that, he leaned forward until her legs parted and he was able to settle himself between them. Her eyes widened and her hands automatically clasped his shoulders for balance.

He released her robe to wrap his long fingers

around her hips, then snugged her that small distance closer until their bodies met, heat on heat. He pushed his hips against her.

In a low growl that was beyond his control, Eric asked, "I've had a hard-on since I walked in the door. Does that feel like disinterest to you?"

Mute, she shook her head while staring into his eyes.

He cupped her breasts again, still outside the robe, and closed his eyes at the exquisite feel of her. "Beautiful. And sexy."

"But . . ."

"I want to see your pretty little breasts, Maggie. I want to see all of you. Will you trust me?"

She stared at his mouth. "Will you kiss me again first?"

He liked it that she wanted his mouth.

Leaning forward, he said, "I'll kiss you everywhere. In time." Her lips parted on a deep sigh as their breaths mingled and he took her mouth. So soft, he thought, amazed that a kiss could feel so incredible, taste so good. He devoured her with that kiss and relished her accelerated breathing. His tongue sank inside and was stroked by hers, hot and damp and greedy. It went on and on and when she relaxed completely, when her open thighs gave up their resistance and she slowly sank back in the chair, half reclining with her legs opened around his hips in a carnal sprawl, he lifted his head.

Watching her, caught by the sight of her velvety dark gaze and swollen mouth, he touched her lapels again. She swallowed, but didn't stop him when he slowly parted the material. As his gaze dipped to look at her, his heartbeat punched heavily inside his chest.

He couldn't imagine a woman more perfectly made. Her rib cage was narrow, her skin silky and pale. Her soft little breasts shimmered with her panting, nervous breaths. Pale pink, tightly pinched nipples begged for his mouth as surely as she had. "Oh, Maggie."

Her hands fell from his arms and flattened on the seat beside her hips, as if she needed to steady herself.

She inhaled sharply, then held her breath as he moved forward to nuzzle against her. Her body, softened only moments before, quickly flexed with tightened muscles and churning need. Teasing, he circled one nipple with tiny kisses, driving himself insane as he resisted the urge to draw her into the damp heat of his mouth, to suck her hard, to sate himself on her.

"Eric . . ."

"Shhh." He flicked her with the very tip of his tongue. "We've got all night."

"I won't last all night."

He chuckled soothingly and switched to the

other breast. Deliberately taking her by surprise, he closed his teeth around her tender flesh and carefully tugged. Her whole body jerked; her hands clasped his head, trying to urge him closer.

From one second to the next, his patience evaporated. Wrapping one forearm around her hips, he anchored her as close as he could get her, pelvis to pelvis, heat to heat, then suckled her into his mouth.

Her groan, long and intense and accompanied by the clench of her body, nearly pushed him over the edge. He drew on her, his head muzzy with the reality of what he was doing, of who he was with. The mere fantasy couldn't begin to compare.

Openmouthed, he kissed his way to her other nipple, greedy for her. She guided him, squirming and shifting, and sighed when he latched onto her breast again as if she needed it, needed him, with the same intensity he felt.

"Do you see," he muttered around her damp nipple, "just how perfect you are?"

She hitched one leg around his hips and hugged him closer. Instinctively, she moved against his rigid erection, seeking what he wouldn't yet give.

Eric slowly pulled away from her, determined on his course.

"Eric . . ." She started to sit up, reaching for him while her legs tightened.

Pushing the robe down to her elbows, trapping her arms; his position between her thighs, combined with her movements, had parted the material over her legs, which now left her virtually naked. The robe framed her body, with the silly belt still tied around her middle. Her belly was adorable, and he kissed it even as he remonstrated with her for her small lie.

"You're not naked, sweetheart." He touched the waistband of her white cotton bikini panties. "Not that I'm complaining, because this is very cute."

"Don't . . . don't make fun of me, Eric."

He managed a grin in spite of the hot throbbing of his body. "Why would I make fun of you? Because of your conservative underwear? I like it."

"Like you like small breasts?"

His gaze met hers. In the pose of a confirmed hedonist, she lounged back, face flushed, body open to the pleasure he'd give her. Her dark hair was mussed, her eyes soft, her lips swollen. He absorbed her near nudity, her innate sexuality, and said gently, "Like I like you."

Her eyes closed briefly, then opened when he dipped one rough fingertip beneath the waistband of her panties and teased her stomach, low enough to just brush her glossy dark curls, high enough to keep her on a keen edge of need.

Her breath came in hungry pants. "Are you going to make love to me, Eric?"

"Absolutely."

"When?"

Situated as he was between her thighs, he could smell her desire, the rich musk of arousal. His nostrils flared. It was a heady scent, mixing with the perfume she'd put on, making his cock surge in his pants, his muscles quiver. "When I think you're ready."

"I'm ready now."

"Let's see." Slowly, he lifted each of her legs and draped them over the arms of the chair. The position left her wide open in an erotic, carnal posture. Eric trailed his rough fingertips up the insides of her thighs, seeing her suck in her stomach, hearing her gasp. Her breasts heaved in excitement and anticipation.

She looked so damn enticing he couldn't resist her. Without warning, he kissed her through the soft damp cotton, his mouth open, his tongue pressing hard. He breathed deeply and felt himself filled with her. He could taste her—and quickly grabbed her hips to hold her steady when she would have lurched away from sheer reaction.

She said his name in a breathless plea.

Her response thrilled him, drove him. He wanted to pull her panties aside so his tongue could stroke her slick naked flesh, heated by her desire, silky wet in preparation for much more than his tongue.

He gave her his finger instead.

Leaning back to watch her, he wedged his large hand inside her panties, stroked her once, twice, then pressed deep. The instant, almost spastic thrust of her hips, her coarse groan, the spontaneous clasp of hidden muscles, told him she liked that very much.

"Jesus, you're tight," he ground out through clenched teeth, struggling to maintain control. "And wet."

"Eric . . ."

He stared at her through burning eyes. "Am I hurting you, babe?"

She groaned, whispered something unintelligible, and her sleek, hot flesh squeezed his finger almost painfully.

"That's it," he encouraged softly, feeling himself near the edge. "Hold on to me." He stroked, slowly pulling his finger out, then thrusting it back in, deep, teasing acutely sensitive tissues, mesmerized by the sight of his darker hand caught between her white panties and pale belly, her glossy black curls damp with excitement.

Eyes closed, body arched, she gave herself up to him as he fingered her, stretching her a bit, playing with her a lot. He pressed his finger deeper, measuring her, then pulled out slowly to tease her taut clitoris, making her entire body shudder.

He wanted all of her at once; he wanted her to feel all the same desperate need he felt. And maybe, just maybe, if he did this well enough, if he made her feel half of what he felt . . . what? She'd give up the presidency of her father's company just to marry him?

Eric hated himself for letting the selfish thought intrude for even one split second. He didn't want her to give up anything. He didn't want her to be forced into choices.

He loved her. *Goddamn it*.

To banish those thoughts, he pulled his hand away and stripped her panties down her thighs. She blinked at him, grabbing the chair arms for balance as he readjusted her and then once again settled himself close. Those long luscious legs of hers looked especially sinful lying open, leaving her totally vulnerable to him, displaying her pink feminine flesh, swollen and slick. Her hips lifted, seeking his touch again. He had to taste her, and leaned forward for one leisurely, deep stroke of his tongue.

Maggie cried out, her entire body jerking in response. Eric was lost.

With a harsh groan he covered her with his body, kissing her mouth deeply, consuming her, taking what he could because he couldn't have it all. Her small body cradled his larger frame perfectly. "I want you so fucking much," he rasped.

"Yes!"

He cupped her breast with a roughness he couldn't control and rocked his hips hard against her, feeling her pulsing heat through his slacks. She was silky soft, warm and female everywhere, and he wanted to absorb every inch of her. With one hand he lifted her soft bottom, grinding himself against her.

"Eric!"

Stunned, he looked at her face and watched her climax, her teeth clenched, her throat arched, her breasts flushed. His heart seemed to slow to a near stop as love consumed him, choking out all other emotions.

She whimpered as he continued to move her against him, more slowly now, carefully dragging out her pleasure, his fingers sinking deep in her soft bottom, letting her ride it out to the last small spasm until finally she stilled and her muscles relaxed.

Limp, eyelashes damp on her flushed cheeks, her lips still parted, she was even more than he'd ever imagined. Eric gathered her close and rocked her gently, attempting to regain control of his own emotions—which were far beyond sexual.

As if each limb were made of lead, Maggie struggled to resettle her legs, locking them around his hips. So slowly he couldn't anticipate what she wanted, she got her arms around his neck, one hand tangled in his hair. Finally her sated, dazed eyes opened.

"Sorry," she muttered in such an endearingly drowsy and somewhat shy voice, he couldn't help but smile with a swell of satisfaction and tenderness.

His hand still held her small backside and he gave her a gentle, cuddling squeeze. "For what, sweetheart?" His tone was soft in deference to the moment.

She studied his face, her own pink, then managed a halfhearted shrug. "Okay. I'm not sorry." She yawned. "Now will you please make love to me?"

How humor could get him while he was so rock hard he could have driven in railroad spikes, he didn't know. But the chuckle bubbled up and he tucked his face into her breasts as he gave in to it.

"Are you laughing at me?"

She didn't sound particularly concerned over that possibility, which made the humor expand.

"Eric?"

Her hand tightened in his hair, causing him to wince. He lifted up, kissed the end of her nose, and grinned. "I'm just happy."

"Why?"

Tenderly, he smoothed a tendril of dark hair behind her ear. "Well, now, I just made Maggie Carmichael come. Why else?"

She snorted, but her face was so hot she looked sunburned. Her hand loosened its grip, her fingers threading through his hair, petting him. "I've wanted you so long, it wouldn't have taken much. Except you kept playing around. . . ."

"Look who's talking."

She raised a brow, but the effect was ruined by another yawn.

"Never mind, sleepyhead. Have I put you out for the night?"

"Absolutely not." She shifted subtly, then whispered, "I'm just dying to feel you inside me, Eric."

"*Jesus.*" He didn't feel like laughing now. Though his legs were shaky, he managed to loosen her hold and stand. He didn't want to make love to her in a damn chair. He wanted her in bed, under him, accepting him.

He reached a hand out to her and when she took it, he hauled her up—and then over his shoulder.

"Eric!"

Flipping the robe out of his way, he pressed his cheek to her hip and kissed her rounded behind. "The bedrooms are upstairs?"

She had both hands latched on to his belt in back, hanging on for dear life. "Yes, but don't you dare. . . . Eric, put me down!"

Instead, he stroked the backs of her thighs with his free hand as he started up the steps. Using just his fingertips, he teased her with light butterfly touches, getting her ready again, keeping her ready.

"Eric . . . *Eric.*" She groaned as he explored her.

Chapter 4

I'm done playing, Eric. Make love to me."

As if he hadn't heard her, Eric strolled into the bedroom and slowly brought her around in his arms. His strength amazed her, not that she was a heavyweight, but considering how boneless she felt right now . . . Of course, he hadn't climaxed.

And she wanted to remedy that as soon as possible.

The second her feet touched the floor, she reached for his belt. Thankfully, he didn't stop her. Instead he began emptying his pants pockets, putting his wallet, a condom, and the sprig of mistletoe he'd removed earlier from the office doorway, onto her nightstand. Seeing the condom and the mistletoe so close together, Maggie shivered.

As she hurriedly worked on his clothes, Eric calmly unknotted the fabric belt still caught around her waist. He finished first and tossed her robe aside. His hands, so incredibly large and warm, settled on her waist, holding her loosely, allowing her to slide his leather belt free and then waiting patiently while she unbuttoned and unzipped his slacks.

"Your hands are shaking," he noted.

She peeked up at him. "I'm excited. I've wanted you . . . well, longer than you can imagine."

"Try me."

To distract him from her words, she abandoned his slacks and quickly began unbuttoning his shirt. The promise of his nudity gave her incentive and her fingers literally flew until his shirt was hanging open.

With a type of reverent awe, she bared his chest. Fingers spread, she ran her hands over his upper torso, absorbing the feel of crisp dark hair, solid muscle, and manly warmth. "I've wanted you since the first time I saw you."

The breathless words took him by surprise, then skepticism narrowed his eyes. "You were barely seventeen, sweetheart. A child."

"Mmmm. And so creative." With the edge of her thumb, Maggie brushed his right nipple and heard his intake of breath. His knees locked. "I got so tongue-tied around you," she whispered, "because at night, alone in my bed, I imagined this very thing. Touching you, having you touch me."

She looked up, saw his flared nostrils, the dark aroused color high on his cheekbones, and she went on tiptoe to kiss his chin, now rough with beard stubble.

Eric caught her wrists as she began a downward descent to his slacks. "You're saying you fantasized about me?"

"From the very beginning." She pulled her hands free and sank to her knees in front of him. She felt like a sexual supplicant, kneeling before him, naked, hot. His erection was a thick ridge plainly visible through his slacks. She leaned forward and pressed her cheek to him, nuzzling. "There's nothing I haven't done to you in my imagination."

"Maggie." One large hand cupped around her head, trembling.

"Lift your foot." He obliged and she tugged off first one shoe and sock, then started on the other. Her face close to his groin, deliberately tantalizing herself—and probably him, given how heavy his breathing had become—she knotted her hands in his slacks and pulled them down.

Eric didn't move as she reached for his snug cotton boxers. More slowly now, savoring the moment, she bared him.

Her breath caught. She'd never seen a fully grown man naked, up close, personal. She'd seen photos, which didn't do the male form justice.

Tentatively, she touched him with just her fingertips and then smiled as he jerked, his erect flesh pulsing, hot. A drop of fluid appeared on the broad head, and she used the tip of one finger to spread it around, testing the texture, exploring him.

Breath hissed out from between his teeth. "That's enough."

Maggie paid him no mind. In her novels, the men always pleasured the women with their mouths; the very idea of it excited her incredibly. But now she wondered why the reverse had never occurred to her. The idea of taking Eric into her mouth, licking him, tasting him, flooded her with heat and doubled her own desire.

"Tell me if I do this wrong," she whispered. And even as he cautioned her to stop, his voice a low, harsh growl, she wrapped one small hand around him to hold him steady. Amazingly, she could feel the beat of his heart in her palm, could feel him growing even more. Her tongue flattened on the underside of his hot, smooth flesh, slowly stroked up and over the tip—and Eric shattered.

She'd barely realized the taste of him, the velvety texture, before he went wild, shaking and gasping. He roughly pulled her to her feet and she found herself tossed on the bed. Before she'd finished bouncing, Eric had kicked his pants off and donned a rubber.

She opened her arms to him and he came down on top of her. Using his knee, he spread her legs wide, then wider still. "I wanted this to be slow," he said through his teeth, reaching down to open her with his fingers, "but I can't wait now."

She started to say she was glad, that she didn't want to wait, but then he thrust hard, entering her, filling her up, and she lost her breath in a rush.

It wasn't at all as she'd imagined, smooth and easy and romantic. Instead, Eric anchored a hand in her hair and held her face still for an all-consuming, wet kiss that made it impossible to breathe, impossible to think. He stroked into her fast and hard. *Deep.* And though she was aware of her own wetness, her own carnal need, the tight friction was incredible.

Her senses rioted over a mix of heated perceptions. There was discomfort, because she was small and inexperienced, but also building pleasure, too acute to bear, because this was Eric and she'd wanted him forever.

Not romantic, but so wonderful, so real and erotic and . . .

Her climax hit suddenly, making her clutch at him, her fingers digging deep into his shoulders, her heels pressing hard into the small of his back. Eric lifted his head, jaw locked tight, eyes squeezed shut, and gave a raw groan as he came.

Through the haze of her own completion, Maggie watched him. She loved him so much, and she wanted him, in every way, always. Seeing his every muscle taut and trembling, his temples damp with sweat, left her feeling curiously tender, softened by the love and the depletion of physical strength.

Eric slowly, very slowly, lowered himself back into her arms. His heart beat so hard against her breast, she felt it inside herself. Threading her fingers through his warm, silky hair, she said, "Eric?"

He gave a small grunt that she supposed might have been a response.

"Will you stay the night with me? Please?" If

he refused, if he left now and this was all she'd ever have, her heart would simply crumble, leaving her empty.

But he didn't refuse her. Instead, his arms tightened and he rolled to his side, bringing her with him. Long seconds led into longer minutes before his breathing ultimately evened out. Idly, he stroked her, her shoulder, her hip, her back. "I'm not going anywhere," he finally said in a rough whisper.

She snuggled closer, letting out the breath she'd been holding.

Eric kissed her forehead and, with a sigh, moved to leave the bed. Enjoying the sight of his naked backside, Maggie watched him go into the bathroom, heard running water, the flush of the toilet, and then he came back. The condom was gone and Eric, in full frontal nudity, his sex now softly nestled in dark hair, was more appealing than she'd ever imagined a man could be. Amazingly, she wanted him again. She licked her lips.

Eric smiled at her as he climbed back into bed. "You little wanton, you," he whispered, and she heard the amusement in his tone. Tucking her into his side and covering them both, he affected a serious tone. "Maggie, this was your first—"

"Yes." She felt a little embarrassed over her inexperience. "I didn't want anyone but you. Not ever."

He absorbed that statement with a heavy silence, then kissed her temple with a gentleness that brought tears to her eyes. "I want you to tell me about this long-hidden admiration you have for me."

Maggie knew her time had come. It took her several seconds to screw up her courage before she could force herself to look up and face Eric. When she did, his hand cupped her cheek and there was a softness in his expression she'd never seen before.

She swallowed hard. "Not an admiration, Eric. Love."

He remained quiet, waiting.

"I've loved you," she declared, "since the first time I saw you. My father knew it, and that's why he left me the company. He believed you wanted it, and he had hoped . . . that is, he thought that perhaps the company would be a lure, to get you to notice me."

Eric stared at her as if someone had just hit him in the stomach. She felt him tense and prayed he'd at least hear her out.

Rushing, hoping to get it all said before she chickened out, she explained, "I don't want the company, Eric. I never have. I wish I'd known what my father was going to do, because I would have stopped him. Not only did it not lure you in, you've been distant since I got the damn controlling stock."

Eric sat up, his expression dumbfounded. Feeling suddenly naked, Maggie clutched the sheet to her throat and came up to her knees. "Eric, I swear we didn't mean to manipulate you. That is, I didn't even know until it was too late—"

"Shh." Eric put a finger to her lips, silencing her. He looked thoughtful, with a frown that wasn't quite annoyance, but rather confusion. "You don't want to run the company?"

Since his finger was still pressed to her mouth, she didn't try to reply. Instead, she shook her head.

Eric left the bed to pace. That was enough of a distraction to make her regret the damn topic. She wanted him back in bed with her. She wanted to do more exploring.

"Now that we're involved," he said, and he looked at her, daring her to challenge his statement, "there's going to be some gossip."

Maggie scrambled off the bed and stood before him, the sheet held in front of her. "I won't let anyone insult you, Eric, I swear!"

A grin flickered over Eric's firm mouth. "Ready to defend me, huh?" He touched her chin. "I can handle gossip, sweetheart. I just don't want it to hurt you."

Heart pounding, she said, "I can handle it—as long as you can."

"Then we're agreed." He cupped her face

and kissed the end of her nose. "Now, about the company . . ."

"You don't have to worry that I'll make you responsible. I'm going to sell my shares. I don't want to be tied to the business so much. I have . . . other interests right now. And Daddy was only trying to make me happy—"

"You're not selling the shares."

Her brows lifted. "I'm not?"

"No. I'll run things for you." His expression was so intent, she squirmed. "If . . ." he said, emphasizing that one word beyond what was necessary, "if you'll marry me."

Maggie caught her breath. Slowly, to make certain she understood, she asked, "You're willing to take the extra shares off my hands—"

"No. The company will remain yours."

"But . . ."

"I won't have people saying you were part of a bargain, Maggie, that I married you for the company. I want it clear that I want you for *you*, not for the added benefits."

"Do you . . . see the company as a benefit?"

He shrugged. "I always assumed I would one day be in charge."

"But you don't want that." Maggie felt swamped in sudden confusion.

"Not true. It's just that I wanted you more."

His voice dropped, became seductive. "Much, much more than any damn company."

"Oh."

Eric sat on the bed and pulled her into his lap—after he tossed the concealing sheet aside. Cupping her breast and watching intently as he thumbed her nipple into readiness, he said, "Just as you say you used to daydream about me, I sure as hell dreamed about you. I planned to make my intentions known after you graduated, except so many things happened then. You lost Drake and inherited a company. Everything got confused. You were missing your father, and I assumed, judging by your competence, that you enjoyed running the company. I thought if I came after you then, you'd never be certain what it was I wanted."

Maggie searched his face, almost afraid to believe. "But you wanted . . . me?"

"God, Maggie." Eric squeezed her tight, and his voice sounded raw with emotion. "I wanted you to the point I about went crazy." He kissed her, then kissed her again.

Big tears gathered in her eyes and she blinked hard to fight them off. "I was so afraid you'd never ever notice me. I tried everything. I thought if I was more sophisticated, if I showed you I wasn't a kid anymore, you'd stop ignoring me."

Eric riffled a hand through her hair. "I love you, Maggie. Exactly as you are, any way you want to be."

Maggie wanted things clarified about the company, but Eric returned to her mouth, and his hand on her breast was lightly teasing, and she felt him hardening against her bottom. She decided further discussion could wait.

Eric rolled over and reached for her, but she wasn't there. A heady contentment had him smiling even before he was completely awake. *Maggie was now his.* Once his eyes were fully open, he saw that it was still night. Where had Maggie gone?

He left the bed, shivering as the cool night air washed over his naked body. Before leaving her bedroom, he pulled on his slacks, but didn't bother buttoning or zipping them.

Creeping silently down the steps and into the living room, he found Maggie at her desk, writing by the lights of the Christmas tree and her laptop. Her beautiful silky hair tumbled around her face, and she'd donned the same soft robe, though sloppily, so that one shoulder was mostly exposed. The twinkling lights of the tree reflected in her big dark eyes while the eerie glow of moon-washed snow outside the French doors framed her in an opalescent halo.

She was absorbed in her writing, oblivious to her surroundings, and didn't notice him. Eric lounged against the wall watching her. So precious. A grin tugged at his mouth as he wondered exactly what scene she was working on now.

The sprig of mistletoe that he'd brought from the office lay on the desk beside her.

"Getting the facts down while they're still fresh in your mind?"

With a yelp, she jerked her head up to stare at him. "Eric! What are you doing down here?"

He strolled toward her, still smiling, filled with contentment and masculine satisfaction. "I was going to ask you the same thing."

She pushed her chair back and stood, then glanced at her laptop. Nervously she began to tidy her desk. She picked up the mistletoe. "I was just . . . too excited to sleep. I figured I might as well get some stuff done."

"Mm-hmm." Eric closed in on her and she turned her back to the desk, her hands clasped at her waist. The mistletoe crushed against her belly. "Ah, now, there's an idea," he said.

Maggie blinked. "What?"

He traced her stomach with one finger, edging underneath her robe. "I read part of your book at the office."

Her mouth fell open, then snapped shut, and she scowled.

"You're incredibly talented."

The scowl disappeared. "I am?"

He nodded. "I can't wait to read the rest of it." Eric met her eyes and asked, "Have you been using me for research?"

"Oh, for crying out loud," she blustered, "I don't—"

"Because I wouldn't mind. At all." He kissed her lips, her throat. Pressing his palm against her beneath the mistletoe, he said, "I kind of like the idea."

A tad breathless, she said, "If you read the book, then you know we haven't done all the things that the characters did."

"But I'd sure like to." His fingers searched her through the chenille. "And the guy in your book reminded me a lot of me."

"Yes." She closed her eyes and sighed. "I've sold three books, Eric. This one will be my fourth. I've written about a doctor, a Navy SEAL, a car salesman, and now a businessman."

Eric froze. "So who were the other guys?"

He watched her lips twitch into a smile. "They're all you, at least in part." Her beautiful brown eyes opened and she stared up at him. "They may not all look like you, but the qualities they have that make them interesting, that make them heroes women want to read about—those I get from you. Those are the things that are most important."

Her words touched his heart. "I do love you, Maggie."

With a crooked smile, she said, "And you like the way I write?"

"I think you're incredible." Slowly, deliberately teasing her, he dropped to his knees. "Will you let me read the rest?"

It took her a breathless moment to say, "When . . . when I'm finished with it."

Eric parted the robe and pressed a kiss to her naked belly, just beneath the mistletoe now crushed in her hands. "And you'll let me run the company for you?"

She dropped the mistletoe. It landed beside Eric's knee. Bracing her hands on the edge of her desk at either side of her hips, she said, "Yes, thank you."

Eric grinned. He used his thumbs to gently part her so he could kiss her where she'd feel it most. "And will you," he asked against her hot flesh, "marry me, sweetheart?"

Her groan was long and loud and unselfconscious. "*Yes.*"

"I've got to hand it to you, Maggie," he said, feeling her legs tense. "This is the best Christmas bonus I've ever gotten."

Epilogue

Eric stood beside Maggie at the Christmas party as she called for everyone's attention. He had no idea what she might do, but he intended to be beside her regardless.

She positively glowed, he thought, watching her dark eyes as she laughed and held up a hand—a hand that sported an engagement ring she'd picked out yesterday. Her hair was pulled back by a red and green headband and she had tiny Christmas bows as earrings. Over her left breast, a miniature Santa head with a blinking red nose drew his attention. He loved it that she'd quickly given up her frumpy suits, and that she was every bit as energetic and enthusiastic as he remembered.

She was especially enthusiastic in bed. Eric had to chase those thoughts away, or be damned with a hard-on for the entire staff to see. He cleared his throat and concentrated on what Maggie was saying.

"This year," she called out, "besides getting the Christmas bonus bucks and a ham, I'm giving everyone a share of company stock."

Eyebrows lifted in surprise and a buzz of hushed conversation filled the hall. Eric stared at Maggie, floored by her declaration.

"It's not much," she explained, "but I didn't want controlling shares, and Eric refused to take them off my hands. So now, he and I are equal partners in the company, and all of you have a stake in it as well. I know my father would have approved."

Heads turned, everyone now staring at Eric. He chuckled, amused at Maggie's way of settling any thoughts of gossip.

"And just for fun, I wanted you all to know"—she flashed the ring, her smile wide—"we're getting married!"

A roar of applause took Eric by surprise. No one seemed the least surprised by her declaration, or suspicious of his motives. Maggie snuggled up against his side and he automatically slipped his arm around her.

Someone, he thought it might have been his secretary Janine, called out, "It's about time," and everyone laughed as if they all agreed.

Maggie put her hands on her hips and pretended to scowl. "How come none of you are surprised?" she asked, laughing.

Janine, accepting the role of leader, stepped forward at the encouragement of her fellow employees. "We've been taking bets," she explained with a smile, "on when the engagement would take place. Everyone could see you were both in love."

"You asked me out," Eric accused her.

"We all did." Janine shrugged, unrepentant. "We thought it might get Maggie moving. And that's why the guys asked Maggie out—"

Eric narrowed his eyes. "Yeah, who did that?" He scanned the crowd, but the men all started whistling and shuffling their feet, trying in vain to hide their humor. Maggie lightly punched Eric in the arm while laughing out loud.

The sound of her laughter never failed to turn him on. He wanted to get the party over with so he could take her home. "We're officially engaged," Eric stated, holding Maggie close, "so you can all keep your distance from her now. Understood?"

The men bobbed their heads, still grinning, while the women smiled indulgently.

Janine made a fist and waved it in the air. "A Christmas engagement. I win!"

Eric shook his head, then tipped up Maggie's chin. "No, I win." He didn't need mistletoe to prompt him. Right there, in front of everyone, he kissed Maggie until her knees went weak—and no one had a single doubt that love had brought them together.

Naughty Under the Mistletoe

Carly Phillips

To Mom and Dad
who made me believe I could do anything.
To Phil
who loves and supports me through everything.
And to Jackie and Jennifer
who make it all worthwhile.

Chapter 1

Antonia Larson fastened the white fur anklet adorned by three silver bells and a green velvet bow, closing the accessory around her leg with a single snap. From the radio on the edge of her desk, a traditional Christmas carol ended and the Bruce Springsteen version of "Santa Claus Is Coming to Town" now reverberated through her small office. Pulling her hat over her head and securing it with bobby pins, she hummed her own off-key rendition of her favorite Christmas tune. She twirled once, pleased with the jingling accompaniment to the gruff voice of The Boss.

If Santa was coming to town, he wasn't going to find Toni being a good girl. Not this year. Not this night. Tonight she was a woman on a mission. A mission to seduce the man she'd been attracted to for too long. She planned to act on what was a physical attraction and indulge in a safe interlude she could easily walk away from when their time together was through. Something Stephan, the firm's confirmed self-proclaimed bachelor, would appreciate and understand.

Because they'd been working closely as colleagues, acting on her desire had been impossible until now—but today had been her last day of work before the long holiday vacation. When she returned after the New Year, she'd be in the new suburban offices of Corbin and Sons. Work and office protocol no longer stood between them. Nothing did except her courage and the nice-girl role she'd played all her life. A role she could afford to let go of, at least this once.

After yet another night of tossing and turning for hours in her lonely double bed, she'd pulled out the December issue of the women's magazine she'd subscribed to on a whim. What other reason could there be since she had no time in her busy lawyer's life to read tips on how to attract men and what turned them on?

But as she'd read the steamy article on naughty versus nice, Toni realized she'd spent the better part of her life as a nice girl, following the rules to get ahead and working overtime to make a good impression. Her two thousand–plus billables over the last few years had put her in a prime position for a promotion. The ailing Mr. Corbin had been thrilled when he'd named her the senior associate to work with the as-of-yet unnamed partner who'd run the new office. She'd never have come this far without performing to perfection. Being naughty had had no place on the ladder to success. Neither had coming on to a man she worked alongside.

But having earned her position, she felt free to act on other, impulsive desires. Then with the onset of the new year, Toni would put Stephan behind her and step back into the stable, secure, independent life she'd created for herself.

If the article were to be trusted, the clichéd adage was true and nice girls finished last. So Toni would just have to be bad. She smoothed her skirt and straightened her hat, giving one last jingle of her bells for good luck. In matters of the hormones and the heart Toni intended to come in first.

No matter how naughty she had to be to accomplish her goal, Toni intended to get her man.

They called this a party? Maxwell Corbin glanced at the dark suits milling about the large conference room. Muffled laughs, discreet corner discussions, and a handshake every now and then to clinch a deal. Not an ounce of fun in sight, he thought and immediately remembered why he'd traded in his SoHo apartment and his family's downtown New York City law firm for a place in the suburbs and his PI office on the Hudson River. An office he'd return to. No matter how happy it would make his father if Max decided to return to the fold, he had to live his own life, his own way. Three years at the family firm had taught him practicing law wasn't it.

As he made for the eggnog across the room, his sneakered foot crushed a stray pretzel, marring the otherwise pristine carpet. Beside him, someone made a toast to an upcoming merger, increased income, and the guaranteed all-nighters to come. Max shook his head in disgust. The only thing worth staying up all night for was sex—something he hadn't had in too damn long, mostly because no woman had interested him enough. But lately he'd begun to wonder what being discriminating and picky had gotten him besides a cold bed at night.

He lifted the ladle to pour himself a drink when the faint ringing of bells caught his attention. He turned toward the sound and the expensively decorated Christmas tree, a pine, lavishly trimmed with white and gold, with dozens of boxes beneath the branches to increase holiday spirit. He stepped to the left so he could see around the tree and caught sight of a dainty elf kneeling over a bulging bag of toys. As she reached inside the large bag, the hem on her miniskirt hiked up higher, revealing black lace beneath white fur trim.

Max swallowed hard. So much for disinterest, he thought wryly. A longer glance as she dug through her huge bag and he discovered the lace ended at mid-thigh. He wondered what she wore beneath that green suit, if the hands-on exploration would be as satisfying as his imagination.

He tried to swallow but his mouth had gone dry. If he had to spend time in the hallowed halls of Corbin and Sons—make that Corbin and Compliant Son, he thought, thinking of his twin—then maybe the pixie in the corner would make his time here worthwhile. He dodged his way around the business suits and headed for the tinsel-laden elf.

On his way, he realized that not only was she the sole focus of his attention, but he was the center of hers. She'd straightened from her chore and looked at him dead-on, heat and something more in her smoky gaze. Drink forgotten, he walked the rest of the way to where she stood. Despite the drone of preoccupied, chattering attorneys, Max felt as if he were approaching her in silken silence.

As he closed in, he raised his gaze from the white fur anklet to her belted, trim waist to her green-eyed stare. Sea-green scrutiny made more vibrant by the interested flush in her cheeks. After promising his father he'd show up at this gig, he'd mentally called the day a bust, but when she pulled him behind the tree, rose onto her booted tiptoes, and touched her mouth to his, he reassessed his opinion.

He'd been kissed before—but he'd never *been* kissed. Not with such intensity and single-minded purpose. She tasted sweet and smelled sensual and fragrant, making both his mind and his body come alive. Her hands gripped his shoulders in a death-lock as her champagne-flavored tongue darted past his willing lips.

She had a potent effect, yet despite it all her touch was endearingly hesitant, turning him on while arousing a fierce protectiveness within him at the same time. He gripped her waist to anchor himself, something she obviously took as a sign of acceptance because a soft but satisfied sigh escaped and he caught the erotic sound with his mouth, deep in his throat. Though he hadn't a clue what he'd done to become the lucky recipient of her attention, he wasn't about to question good fortune. He'd rather make more of his own.

He began an arousing exploration, mating his tongue with hers in a prelude she couldn't misinterpret or mistake. And obviously she didn't. Her head tipped backward and she welcomed the onslaught of his roving tongue and hands. His fingers locked onto her petite waist and he pulled her forward, her breasts flush with his chest, her hips brushing his.

Such close contact with his elf had him aching for more and he sucked in a startled breath, inhaling deeply. The scent of pine assaulted his senses and reminded him of their surroundings and the possibility that despite the barrier of the Christmas tree, they might have an audience of attorneys taking copious notes. With regret he raised his head and took a safe step back from temptation. Emerald eyes glazed with desire stared back, an engaging smile on her well-kissed lips.

"Mistletoe," she said in a husky voice, pointing upward.

He glanced at the bare ceiling. So she had

passion as well as a desperate need for an excuse. A grin tipped the edges of his mouth as he wondered what other surprises this mystery lady had in store. "Whatever you say."

She touched her lips with shaking fingertips. "I say you're not *him*. You're nothing like Stephan."

Kind of her to point out something he'd been told hundreds of times before. But she'd spoken low, more to herself than to him, and not with the well-aimed need to hurt, the way the information had been used against him in the past.

Her gaze darted from his worn basketball sneakers, up the length of his dark denim jeans, and focused on his face. "In the dim lighting and from a distance you kind of looked like him." He saw as well as heard her searching for answers. "The same dark hair and piercing blue eyes, though yours are somewhat warmer." A glimmer of passion infused her voice. "Similar dimple but yours is deeper." She reached out with the same hesitant determination he'd sensed behind the kiss.

Her touch burned him straight to his soul.

"And when he works weekends, he . . . dresses . . . like . . . you." She jerked her hand away from the same fire consuming him.

Max was surprised to learn Stephan ever veered away from conservative suits and ties.

Maybe he and his twin had come from the same egg after all. Maybe they had more in common than either of them let on. And maybe they *could* be friends as well as brothers. The thought arose, not for the first time in ages, but it was the first time he considered acting on the impulse.

He had his elf to thank for revealing the surprising similarities and possibilities. *His* elf. Funny how proprietary he'd become in such a short span of time. But it wouldn't be funny if she had any kind of relationship with his twin, and based on that hell of a kiss, the odds tipped against Max.

"Since it's not the weekend, I should have known," she murmured. Scrutiny complete, she settled her stare on his New York Rangers jersey, an obvious attempt to avoid his gaze. Then she folded her arms across her lush chest, chewing on her bottom lip as the enormity of her mistake obviously set in.

He remembered the feel of those curves pressed intimately against him, recalled the sweetness of her mouth, and he struggled not to groan aloud. "Something against the Rangers?" he asked, seeking the more mundane.

She shook her head, her button nose crinkling in answer. "I don't have time for basketball."

"Hockey."

"Whatever. But baseball's another story. How 'bout those Mets?" A twinkle sparkled in her glorious eyes.

Apparently she'd been giving him a hard time and was probably as big a sports fanatic as he, something he'd never expected to find in a woman.

"Hard to believe a Corbin would wear a jersey to an office party, though." Her brows rose in surprise.

On any other woman, the gesture would remind him of his judgmental federal court judge mother. But on *her,* the otherwise critical display indicated curiosity and interest, not disdain. "You've got that right. But I'm not a typical Corbin." He felt the welcome tug of a smile.

She inclined her head, her silky black hair brushing her shoulders much the way he'd like it caressing his skin. "Tell me something I don't know."

Once again, her trembling fingers touched her mouth, this time tracing the outline of her reddened lips before she caught herself and stepped around the tree, reaching for the first gift-wrapped package she could find. He allowed her escape for the moment, watching the sexy sway of her hips in retreat. And in that instant, her words immediately after that mind-blowing kiss came back to him. *You're not him. You're nothing like Stephan.*

She'd kissed him and known instantly. And she wasn't all that upset and she definitely wasn't unaffected. The thought pleased him. Though Max could never compete with his twin as a Corbin son, he'd obviously made headway with . . . his brother's woman? His gut clenched at the thought.

"Hello, Max." Stephan walked up beside him.

"Hey, little brother." Catching the scowl on his twin's face, Max grinned, feeling on safe, sibling-sparring ground. "'Little brother' is a figure of speech. You know that. But you also know I got sprung first."

"Three minutes isn't enough to hold it over me our entire lives," Stephan said with characteristic grumbling. "But I'm glad you made it." He surprised Max by slapping him on the back. Obviously his brother wasn't threatened by his father's summons of his wayward, prodigal son. Another reason for Max to suddenly hold out hope he'd leave this party with more than he'd walked in with.

At the very least, a renewed connection to his twin and at best a new woman in his life? Possible, Max thought, unless—he glanced at his brother. "Who's the elf?"

Stephan folded his arms across his chest and glanced around the tree to where the woman who'd kissed Max senseless now tried to feign interest in her bag of toys and not the Corbin brothers. Max stifled a smile.

"Who, Toni?" Stephan asked.

"Toni." Max tested the name on his tongue, liking the sound as well as the incongruity of a man's name on such a feminine creature.

"She's an associate—something you'd know if you didn't make yourself so scarce."

His brother was right. Other than the obligatory holidays at home, Max avoided family situations—especially family business functions like this one—if only because they were always fraught with tension between himself and his parents.

"Any interest?" Max asked, ignoring his brother's jibe but still needing to lay other cards on the table.

Stephan shook his head. "Maybe when she first started working here, but that was a while ago. And once we became colleagues and friends . . ." He waved his hand in dismissal. "No interest."

It was obvious to Max that she didn't feel the same—at least she hadn't before kissing the wrong twin, but no point in informing his brother now. "You sure?"

"No interest. Not that way." Stephan glanced

at him, surprised but obviously certain. "Field's clear."

And so were his brother's words. Nothing stood between Max and his elf.

He turned, determined to stake his claim, but she was talking with a female colleague, and then without warning the conference room was overrun with scampering, chattering children. "What's this?" Max asked over the din.

Stephan laughed. "*This* is Toni's contribution to the annual firm Christmas party. We always made a cash donation to a charity, but she insisted we do something more personal, too. Now we buy gifts for the kids at one of the local women's shelters and Santa hands them out—with her help."

"Santa?"

"Dad. But not this year. He'll be here but the doctor's banned him from anything too stressful like picking up the kids and putting them on his lap. At least until next year."

A twisting pain lanced through Max. "You sure?"

"That he'll be around till next year?" Stephan asked, finishing Max's unspoken question in a way only a twin could. "I'm sure. Spend some more time with him and you will be, too."

Max had seen the older man in the hospital and again when he'd been released, but they'd never been alone long enough to get into serious conversation. Yet apparently the stroke had prompted a renewal in the older man's determination to get Max back into the family firm, because he'd been summoned here by his father, who claimed he had an offer Max couldn't refuse.

"He's determined enough for four men," Stephan said.

"Swell." Determined to stick around and determined to get his way with his one ornery son. Well, one out of two wouldn't be bad. Max glanced at his twin, knowing he had to be honest about not wanting to take over in the office, or in his brother's hard-worked-for domain. "Hey bro, you should know I have no intention of coming back—"

Stephan cut him off with a slug to the shoulder. "*I* know. The only one you have to convince is Dad."

Max nodded. His brother was obviously secure in his place and position within the firm and the family. One potential problem taken care of.

He looked over. His elf—Toni—was kneeling down with kids beside her, tickling one, laughing with another. Not only did she have an altruistic streak but from the looks of things she was a natural-born nurturer, too. Add that to her sexy-as-hell appearance and her knockout kiss and Max knew he'd found a gem. Getting to know her would be a real pleasure.

"Who's replacing Dad as Santa this year?" Max asked.

"Even cash couldn't sway any of these uptight jokers to do the job and I wasn't sure I'd make it on time, so Toni's handing out the gifts herself," Stephan said.

"Really."

His brother chuckled aloud. "You sound awfully pleased. Aren't you too old to be telling Santa what you want for Christmas?"

Max grinned. "Hell, no. Especially not if it'll let me get close to his sexy emissary." And as soon as the children were finished, he planned to tell Santa's helper exactly what he wanted for Christmas.

Chapter 2

Toni was one part mortified and two parts completely turned on. She was in a sweat that owed nothing to the crowded, overheated room and everything to the man watching her out of the corner of his eye. With hindsight and the rush of adrenaline to act on impulse gone, she saw the differences in the brothers more clearly. This man had slightly longer though equally black hair, and razor stubble gave him a more rugged, less clean-cut appearance. He exuded a raw masculinity that appealed to her on a deeper, more carnal level. One she hadn't known existed inside her until that kiss.

That kiss. Toni hugged her arms around her chest, as if she could hold tight to the feelings he inspired. As always, she forced herself to take an honest look at herself, her actions, and the situation. She couldn't deny the truth. At a crossroads, about to embark on a new professional life, she couldn't afford more than a one-night stand, no matter how out of character it was. She'd thought Stephan Corbin was the perfect man on whom to test her feminine wiles, but she'd been wrong. Whatever attraction she'd felt for Stephan paled in comparison to what she'd experienced under the nonexistent mistletoe with his twin. And darned if she didn't want an instant replay.

But with the onslaught of children from the shelter, she had no choice but to wait. In the meantime, she continued the cat-and-mouse game of eye contact he'd begun earlier. Her heart beat frantically in her chest and anticipation flowed through her veins.

"Only two more kids, Toni," Annie, her secretary, whispered in her ear.

"I don't know whether to say thank goodness because I'm beat or thank goodness because even one child here is one too many." She ought to know, having spent more than one night in a shelter as a child.

"How about thank goodness so you can go play get-to-know-you with the Corbin twin?"

Toni felt the heat rise to her cheeks. Had Annie seen that consuming kiss behind the tree?

"He hasn't taken his eyes off you since you sat down in this chair."

Toni shifted in her seat to accommodate the next little girl. "Did you know Stephan had a brother?" she asked Annie.

"No, but I wish I had, at least before you nailed him for yourself. I've got to run. I have a date. Have fun tonight," she whispered on a laugh and walked away before Toni could respond.

The last two children and their requests for Santa went quickly. Toni kept her mental list of extra things to send over to the shelter from Santa and soon the kids, their chaperones, and the gifts were bundled up and on their way. She started to rise, knowing she still had an office to pack before the night was through.

"Not so fast."

She recognized the seductive voice that rumbled from behind.

She curled her hands around the arms of the office chair she'd appropriated, steadying herself with a firm grip. "Something I can do for you?"

"Since you have a special relationship with the big man in the red suit I was hoping you could relay a wish." His strong fingertips brushed her hair back from her face and around her ear, strumming across her skin with perfect precision.

Her stomach fluttered with longing and she forced an easy laugh. "Aren't you too old to believe in Santa?"

"Aren't you too young not to?"

"I'm dressed like one of his elves. Doesn't that tell you something about who and what I believe in?" And right now she believed in this man—and anything he said or did.

She tipped her head to the side and found herself sharing breathing space, close enough to kiss him if she desired. And she did, badly. She'd never experienced anything as strong as her immediate attraction to this stranger.

"It tells me some. But I know too little about you and I intend to change that." He walked around and eased himself onto the arm of her chair, not on her lap but close enough to increase her growing awareness.

His hip brushed her arm and her body heat shot up another ten degrees. She glanced around at the thinning group of people.

Though she and her companion didn't seem to be garnering added attention, Toni was still aware of this being a place of business.

Even if she had temporarily forgotten once she'd gotten him behind the tree, they were in full view of the masses now. "I'm not Santa Claus so there's no lap-sitting involved," she warned him.

He bent closer. "I'll accept those barriers . . . for now."

She inhaled a shaky breath. His masculine scent, a heady mix of warm spice and pure man, tempted her to throw caution aside. Before she could lose common sense she grasped the one thread of the conversation she could remember. "So what can I tell Santa you desire . . . I mean want. What can I tell Santa you want?"

She'd caught her phrasing, an obvious extension of her thoughts and needs, and attempted a too-late retraction. But the word "desire," once spoken, hovered in the air, teasing, arousing, and building upon the electricity arcing between them.

"I know what you meant." He laughed and the deep sound both eased and aroused her in ways she didn't understand. "I also know what you want and it's the same thing I do."

A tremor shook her hard. "And what would that be?"

"To finish what we started under the so-called mistletoe."

A rousing round of applause erupted around them, interrupting their banter and his huskily spoken words. Despite the beat of desire thrumming inside her, she forced herself to look for the cause of the stir. She glanced up and saw Mr. Corbin, the firm's senior partner—Stephan and his twin's father—standing in the doorway. *His twin.* But beyond the obvious resemblance Toni drew a sudden blank.

Oh, Lord. For as quickly as they'd connected, she didn't even know his name.

He brushed his knuckles across her cheek in a gesture more tender and caring than overtly sexual. She could have melted at his feet. And then there was the heat rushing through her body. She felt on edge, the desire inside her out of control.

He rose to his feet. "I've got to go greet the old man but no way are we finished."

She bit the inside of her cheek. When she'd decided to go after Stephan, the firm's bachelor, she'd known nothing long-term could come of it. She'd just wanted to enter the new year feeling good and knowing she could get the man she thought she desired, if just for a brief time. But she'd kissed the wrong brother—or the right brother depending on her perspective—and knowing nothing about him, all bets were off.

So she could continue her bold act and see where things led or she could run, something she'd seen her mother do too many times. Toni Larson didn't run.

"Oh, we're finished all right." She licked at her dry lips. "At least until you tell me your name."

"It's Max." Amusement mingled with desire in his blue-eyed gaze.

She grinned. "'Bye, Max."

He shook his head. "Only until later, Toni." His words held certainty, his voice the promise of sharing more than just an introduction. With a last glance, he reluctantly turned and walked away.

She watched as he approached the older man and witnessed what was so obviously a reunion between a father and a son he loved deeply. A lump rose to her throat. Looking at Max, Toni saw concern and love cross his handsome features, no hint of the playful man in sight. Apparently this reunion was emotional for both men.

But as Max broke from his father's arms, he said something light enough to make Stephan laugh. Then he turned and, from across the room, his compelling gaze met hers and he treated her to a sexy wink. One that assured her he hadn't forgotten her or his promise of seeing her later.

Her stomach curled in anticipation and searing heat assaulted her senses. She shook her head, amazed. Not only had she been naughty, she'd most certainly gotten her man. Just not the man she'd expected. Fate and irony were at work tonight. She touched her fingers to her lips and imagined the feel of his mouth working magic over hers, his warm breath and his masculine scent wrapping her in seductive heat.

She let out a breathless sigh, knowing the night she'd desired was about to get much, much hotter.

Max hadn't wanted to leave Toni's side, not for an instant, which he supposed told him something about the strength of his attraction to a woman he barely knew. An attraction he wanted to explore further.

After spending time and discussing everything *but* business with Max, the older man had grown tired and said he'd see Max at home tomorrow. He just hoped the truce they'd begun to forge today lasted once Max told his father that no offer, no matter how supposedly enticing, could coax him back into the family firm. The most the older Corbin could expect from Max was a loving son who'd always be there for him. Max hoped it would be enough.

But before he had to deal with tomorrow, he had tonight ahead of him and he looked forward to every last minute. He walked down the darkened hallway, lit only by lights from some occupied offices, and stopped by the door his brother had told him belonged to Toni.

Light shone from beneath the partially closed door and the low strains of music sounded from inside. Anticipation and arousal beat heavy inside him as he let himself in. Toni was emptying her office, packing boxes and singing while she worked.

The woman couldn't carry a tune to save her life. Max folded his arms across his chest and grinned. "You can serenade me anytime."

She yelped and jumped. "You shouldn't sneak up on me like that."

He stepped forward, moving closer. With each step he took toward her, she inched back until she hit the wall, looking up at him with wide eyes. "What are you doing?"

"What you asked. Making my presence known."

"As if I could miss it," she said wryly.

"But you're afraid of me."

She shook her head in denial but he backed off anyway. He wanted this woman in many and varied ways but frightened wasn't one of them.

"You don't scare me . . . Max." His name fluttered off her lips. Then as if to prove her point, she held her hand out for him to shake. "And it's nice to officially meet you."

"Likewise." He eased his hand inside hers. Warm and soft, her skin caressed his coarser flesh.

"You just surprised me," she said in a husky voice.

"A good surprise, I hope."

"Definitely that. So why are you here?"

"I was hoping to talk you into going for dinner."

She bit down on her lower lip. "What if I have plans?"

He propped a shoulder against the wall beside her. "Break them," he said with more confidence than he felt. His biggest fear was that she'd blow him off before they had a chance to explore what was between them.

"Convince me." Her teasing smile invited him to do just that.

He curled his fingers around her hand and pulled her toward him, wrapping one arm around her waist and holding her other hand out in front of them. "Let's dance."

Her eyes opened wide. "You're kidding?"

"Do you see me laughing?" He pulled her flush against him and swept her around the small office in time to the beat of the music. He had no idea what had come over him except he had no intention of losing her now.

She anchored her hand around his back for support, molded her body to his and let go. He felt it in the sway of her hips and saw it in the sassy tilt of her head. She was enjoying herself and he was glad.

His body couldn't ignore her lush curves and his groin hardened, unsatisfied with a single dance. But Max wasn't in this for a one-night stand. He was a man who'd spent his life trusting his own instincts and he wasn't about to question his gut now. He wanted much more than sex with this woman and for Max that was a first.

She tilted her head back. "You've got good moves."

"I give my partner all the credit."

Her smile was nothing short of incredible. "Is that what I am?"

"You tell me." He turned her once and stilled. They were so close, their warm breath mingled. So aware of one another, he thought, as he stared into her expectant eyes.

Toni's legs shook beneath her and she tightened her grip on the only available means of support—Max's waist and hand. Then she waited as he lowered his mouth to hers, slowly, surely, his blue-eyed stare never wavering until his lips touched hers.

Their first kiss had been spontaneous, unplanned, and yes, she admitted to herself, a bit desperate. But this was so much more. He took his time, his tongue delving and discovering the deep recesses of her mouth, learning *her,* not once rushing the moment.

Her stomach curled in response to the drugging kiss, much the way her fingers curled into his skin.

His lips slid gently over hers, making the most of the moisture they generated together. Strong yet gentle, he took control, mastering the moves that made her sigh into him and spin dizzily out of control. Toni needed to participate on equal footing and she traced the outline of his strong lips with her tongue and reveled in his uninhibited verbal response. He was a man who not only expressed his physical desire but was bold enough not to hide his emotional reaction. The masculine groan found an answering pull deep inside Toni, in a place she'd kept hidden, uncharted until now.

Without warning, he pulled back, leaning his forehead against hers, his breathing rough in her ear. But the intimacy of continued body contact felt both good and right. Teetering on an emotional precipice, Toni shook deep inside.

"Have I convinced you yet?" he asked.

"Convinced me of what?" She was out of breath, stunned by the intensity of the short but extremely emotional encounter. She couldn't call it just a kiss, not when he'd engaged her heart and soul in every move he'd made. Did he really expect her to think clearly now?

"I am so glad to see I can make you forget everything but me." He laughed, a husky, tender sound that sent ribbons of warmth curling through her. "I asked you to break dinner plans to go out with me. You said I should convince you, remember?"

He reached out and traced the outline of her moist lips with his fingertip, reminding her of the kiss and all that had passed between them. "So did I convince you?"

Her tongue darted out, coming into contact with his salty skin.

He sucked in a startled breath and he met her gaze. "I'm going to take that as yes," he warned.

He could take her anywhere, anytime, but she wasn't about to tell him that. Instead she cleared her throat and straightened her shoulders. "Dinner sounds great. But I can guarantee you that without a reservation there's not a place around that doesn't have at least an hour or more wait."

Dinner, reservations, Toni hoped everyday

conversation would center her somehow, but after this interlude, she doubted her feet would touch the floor again tonight.

"Then it's a good thing I have an in at someplace special. You ready?"

"Dressed like this?" She glanced down at her green tights and fur-lined skirt and wished she hadn't come to work dressed as an elf but had changed at the office instead.

He took in her outfit, one she hadn't thought of as sexy until she saw herself in his glazed eyes. "The place I have in mind doesn't have a dress code."

"How about a people code?" She pulled at her hat until the pins gave way and she tossed it aside.

He slid his fingers over a long strand of her hair. "Everyone's allowed, bar none, including elves." His eyes twinkled with mischief. "Just leave the reindeer outside."

"Cute."

"No, I'm serious. The place is called Bar None and you're more than welcome. My old college roommate owns the joint. So will you come with me?"

In his eyes, she saw the same hope and anticipation alive inside her and grabbed for her courage. "Okay, Max. Lead the way."

◆ ◆ ◆

Max had a hard time concentrating on driving with Toni beside him. She shifted in her seat and he felt the heat of her stare.

"While you were twirling me around my office . . ." she began.

"And kissing you senseless . . ." He couldn't help but remind her of what he'd never forget.

Toni shot Max a wry glare. "You didn't mention this place was in the boonies."

"That's because you didn't ask."

She held her hands out in front of the heater, but he doubted she needed the warmth. He pulled his truck past the train station, lit by traditional colored Christmas lights that gave the place a festive look, much like the rest of the smaller town. Another half-mile down, Max turned into a private street and pulled the car into a gravel parking lot. The Bar None, an old-fashioned pub and restaurant, was in the same upstate town where he lived and worked, a good forty-minute car ride from New York City.

"Forget me asking. I think you were more afraid I'd say no."

He grinned. "That, too." After their second kiss, the one where they'd connected on too many levels to count, Max hadn't been about to lose her by mentioning a little detail like distance. "I gave you the chance to turn around, didn't I?"

She laughed. "While you were doing fifty-five, yeah, you did."

He'd then proceeded to find out as much about his elf as possible, discovering she was at a turning point in her life. Feeling overburdened and overworked, she had the new year pegged as a fresh start. She hadn't elaborated and he'd given her the freedom to reveal as much or as little as she desired.

Though he didn't want to spook her by getting too serious too fast, Max knew he had every intention of being part of her new beginning. He shifted to park.

"So your friend owns this place?" she asked, glancing around her.

He nodded.

"Gorgeous decorations."

Max took in the icicle lights dripping from the shingles and overhang along with the colored lights circling the surrounding shrubbery, seeing the setting he viewed daily from her new, awed perspective. "They are incredible." And so was she.

"How do you plan on explaining me? My outfit, I mean." She laughed, a lilting but embarrassed sound that reminded him of her jingling bells. Those she'd removed somewhere during their ride up the West Side Highway and they lay in the center console.

"I'll just tell him you're Santa's helper." He turned in his seat and reached for her hand.

She tipped her head to one side, a wry smile curving her lips. "And you think he'll buy that?"

He shook his head. "Doesn't matter to me what Jake believes. But it matters to me what you believe." He'd only known her a few hours but the connection he felt with her was real.

Her lashes fluttered upward as she met his gaze. Deep and compelling, her eyes settled on him. Did she know? Understand? Feel the same overwhelming attraction and need as he felt pulsing through his body at this very moment?

Max wondered. He'd never fallen hard and fast for a woman he barely knew, but he had now. Feeling vulnerable wasn't something he was used to and he suddenly needed proof she felt the same. "Tell me something. Since you brought it up, what was behind the elf outfit?" He'd heard his brother's version. He wanted to hear hers.

She glanced away. "I was just spreading some holiday cheer."

"Maybe that's part of the reason, but I doubt it covers everything. And before we go into that crowded bar, I want to know more about you." Something that would show him she trusted him. Something to prove to him that this . . . thing . . . between them wasn't all one-sided.

She bit down on her lower lip. "What did Stephan tell you about me? And don't tell me you didn't ask."

He laughed, admiring both her intuition and nerve. "That you organized the children's visit to Santa and the gifts. That's all."

She inclined her head. "And you want to know why."

He shook his head. "I want to know *you*."

Looking into his eyes, Toni believed him. Though nothing had been said aloud, somewhere between kissing him and . . . well . . . kissing him, a sense of caring had developed, too. They didn't know nearly enough about one another but he was giving her the opportunity to change that.

She'd never admitted her past to a man before, never felt close enough—yet she felt that closeness now. The vulnerability she normally associated with opening up to a man was nowhere to be found. Considering she wasn't planning anything more than the here and now, the notion rattled her. Badly.

His hand brushed her cheek and remained there. "You can trust me, sweetheart."

As she turned her head so his palm cupped her face, a renewed sense of rightness swept through her. "I spent my childhood in and out of a women's shelter," she admitted. "Whenever my mother got up the courage to leave, we'd find one my father didn't know about. Then when things got rough, she'd go back to him and it would start all over again."

He let out a low growl. "That shouldn't happen to any child."

"Exactly." She shrugged self-consciously. "Which explains the Christmas party and my elf outfit."

"Which explains my attraction to you," he murmured.

"You have a thing for little women dressed in green?"

"You make yourself sound like a Martian." He burst out laughing but sobered fast. Nothing about what she'd revealed was funny. "Actually, I have a thing for a certain raven-haired beauty with a big heart."

She shook her head, flushed. "Don't give me that much credit. Really. It's all very self-serving. When I got out of high school, I swore I'd finish my education somehow. No matter how many student loans I had to take, I promised myself I'd find a way to be self-supporting so I'd never run out of options like my mother had."

"And you've accomplished that."

"With a little unexpected help," she said, gratitude evident in her tone. "I found out when my mother passed away she'd taken out an insurance policy. Enough money to cover my education—after the fact. So my loans are paid off, but I spent years working like a demon for that sense of security."

"But you've got that now."

"Most definitely." She turned away, reaching for the door handle. "I'm starving," she said, changing the subject.

Obviously she didn't want to take things too quickly, but Max made a mental note to find out more. "Toni, wait."

She glanced over her shoulder.

"One more question."

"Yes?"

"You thought you were kissing my brother."

Even in the darkened car he could see the heat of a blush rise to her cheeks. "Mistaken impulse," she said.

"Any feelings behind it?"

"Just one."

He waited a beat before she finally finished.

"Regret."

Max felt as if he'd been kicked in the gut. Until she turned completely and scooted over in the seat, so close he could smell her perfume. "I regret that you obviously think there was something going on between me and Stephan. Or that I have feelings for your brother other than friendship."

"Don't you? You initiated that kiss. I have a hard time believing it was born of feelings of friendship." Despite the fact that she'd let him into her heart and the painful parts of her past, she'd yet to openly admit her interest in him.

"This is so humiliating and I'm going to sound so desperate." She laughed and shook her head. "I thought I was interested in your brother and I acted on the opportunity." She shrugged. "Turns out I was wrong." Those velvet green eyes met his. "I thought I wanted Stephan—until the second I kissed you."

Max had his answer and let out a ragged breath of air. She wanted him, too. So, he thought, let the night begin.

Chapter 3

Hey, Detective, how's it going?"

"Just fine, Milt."

Detective? Max had grabbed Toni's hand and she followed him through the crowd at the bar to the back of the paneled pub, decorated with silver and green tinsel along the top of dark wood. There was no way he could hear her above the din so she waited until they'd reached their destination before yanking on his hand and capturing his attention. "You're a detective?"

"Private investigator. Why?"

"No special reason. I just had no idea what you did for a living."

"And now you do." He turned toward the bar. "Hey, Jake, give me a round of . . ."

Max turned toward Toni and she shrugged. "Whatever you're having is fine."

"Two Coronas."

The man he'd called Jake, a light-haired man about the same age and height as Max, nodded in return. "Hey, Brownie," Jake called to someone across the room. "Get your ass up and give the detective his table."

Max laughed. "I have a standing seat in the corner." He gestured toward a high table with two barstools where an older man was clearing out.

"He doesn't have to give up his seat for us," Toni said.

"He damn well does. If we don't boot him out of here, he drinks too much. He's too lazy to stand on his feet all night. This way he'll go home and sleep it off." Max caressed her face with his knuckles. "Trust me. I've been through this routine before."

"You've booted him out for his own good? Or booted him out to make room for you and another woman?" She bit the inside of her cheek, hating herself for asking but needing the answer just the same.

"There are no *other* women."

Toni liked the answer, but couldn't help wondering if he was telling her what he thought she wanted to hear. Seconds later, he dispelled her concerns by cupping her cheeks in his palms and lowering his lips for a seductive, heated kiss. One that left her gasping for air, unable to think, and the subject of intense speculation, she realized, as he lifted his head.

The stares of onlookers turned into a slow round of applause and more than one whistle of approval. "Way to go, Detective."

Embarrassed, she lowered herself onto the nearest barstool with shaking knees, just as Jake arrived with their drinks.

"You sure do know how to make an entrance, Corbin. Now are you going to introduce me to your lady?"

"*His* lady?"

Jake laughed. "I've owned this place nearly ten years and he's never brought a woman here before. If you can think of another label, just let me know."

Max joined his friend's amused chuckling. "See? Proof to back up my claim. Jake Bishop meet Toni . . ."

"Larson," she said, extending her hand before his friend realized how little they knew about each other.

"Nice to meet you, Toni." Jake swung a towel over his arm. "Can I get you two something to eat? My burgers are the best." Without waiting for an answer, he disappeared into the kitchen.

"Modest guy."

Max dragged the empty stool close to hers and swung himself into it. "He can afford to be full of himself. Look at this place. It's a gold mine. Of course it is the only bar for miles."

She nodded. "And one where you've got your own table and everyone seems to know you. Do you call this place home?" Toni liked the rustic, comfortable decor. The place emitted warmth and a down-home atmosphere that welcomed its customers and she could see Max spending his free time here.

"As a matter of fact I do." He gestured upward. "I rent the place upstairs."

"Really." She leaned forward and rested her chin on her hands. "And here your friend said you don't make it a habit of luring unsuspecting women to your lair."

He shook his head, his gaze never leaving hers. "I haven't lured you anywhere you didn't want to go. And if you want me to drive you back to the city after dinner, I will."

Her heart beat out a rapid crescendo in her

chest. She didn't want to go anywhere without him. They'd just met tonight but she'd never felt so much so fast. "And if I don't?" she asked softly.

Max leaned closer. "If you don't want to go back, then you stay with me."

His warm breath tickled her cheek and she realized she could easily fall hard for this man. All six feet of him put her at a petite disadvantage, yet for a woman who prided herself on her independence, she had to admit she liked his overpowering air and the heady way he made her feel.

Enough to consider spending the night?

"Burgers, folks." Jake arrived, interrupting the electric current of awareness running between them. After serving them their meals, Jake grabbed a chair and dragged it over.

Max eyed his friend warily. Jake never knew when to butt out. Max ought to resent Jake's intrusion, but hell, the man was a bartender. Being nosy was his business, and besides, Max needed a break or else he'd grab Toni's hand and drag her upstairs to his bed—the one thing he wanted and the last thing he ought to do. He needed to build on the tentative start they'd made, not rush into a one-night stand. Which wasn't to say he wouldn't follow her lead, Max thought.

"So where'd you two meet, a costume party?" Jake asked, then gestured to the food in front of them. "Go 'head and eat."

Max rolled his eyes. "We met in the city."

"I work with his brother," Toni explained.

"She's a lawyer?"

"Not a typical one," Max said, knowing Jake was already questioning why he'd fall for one of what Max had always labeled a stuffy breed.

"This true?" Jake asked.

"I guess." Toni shrugged. "At least no more than he's a typical Corbin."

"You two seem to have a handle on each other."

Not nearly well enough, Max thought. Not yet.

Jake leaned forward in his seat, ready for more conversation. "Sounds like a match made in heaven to me."

"You realize the place is emptying out while you're hanging out here?" Max asked.

"Are you looking to get rid of me?"

"Could I if I tried?"

Toni laughed. "You two sound like brothers."

Max shrugged. "Live with a guy for four years and you get the urge to kill him every once in a while."

"The man speaks the truth." Jake leaned back and took in the emptying bar. "Less money, more family time. I don't know whether I love or hate the holidays."

"He closes early during the week before Christmas," Max explained.

"That's nice."

Max wondered if he mistook the wistful look in Toni's eyes when Jake mentioned family time and holidays in the same breath. Recalling her childhood, he doubted he was off base and he wanted the opportunity to replace older, sadder memories with newer, happier ones.

"Well, you two be good." Jake turned to Toni and winked. "I'm going to start wrapping things up for the night."

For the next hour, while Jake cleared out the remaining customers and then locked the door behind Max and Toni, promising to return early for a real cleanup, Max ate and watched Toni do the same. He wasn't a man prone to talking about himself but she had him explaining the types of cases he handled and describing the thrill of working in the field as opposed to behind a desk or in a courtroom. To his surprise, she didn't turn her nose up or question his choices. If anything, she not only approved but seemed to envy his ability to walk away from the pressure and grind to do what he enjoyed.

Max studied her. Now that she'd paid off her student loans, she could afford to start making choices out of enjoyment and not necessity. He wondered if she even realized she had that option, but before he could delve deeper into her life, the conversation detoured yet again.

But no matter what they discussed Max found himself drawn to her. Not just because they shared a passion for take-out Mexican food and Rollerblading in fresh air, but because she was unique: She was a woman who made him want to open up, a woman who interested him so much he wanted to know more about her life, and a woman who accepted the choices he made. A woman he desired not just in his bed, though that was a given, but in his life, to see where things led.

And if her footwork was any indication, she wanted the same thing. She'd obviously let her elf boots fall to the floor and she'd brushed her foot against his leg once too many times for comfort or accident. The light flush in her cheeks and her inability to look him head-on told him she didn't find her overt moves easy. But he was grateful for her interest and he intended to keep things light and fun—to give her space to decide how far she wanted to take things, knowing he wouldn't accept just tonight. It would be *her* decision to stay or go, no matter how much his body throbbed with growing need.

Conversation became more difficult as she

intentionally massaged his calf with the arch of her foot, inching upward beneath the table.

He leaned closer. "You're a naughty girl, Toni." He captured her foot between his legs, stilling her arousing movements.

It was either stop her or let her continue her upward climb, in which case their evening would end before it ever began. And with the bar empty and Jake gone, Max would much rather start their time together fresh and new.

"Being naughty's the whole point, Max."

"You sound like a woman with a plan." He paused, thinking of their unusual meeting. "And it started with that kiss."

"You're astute. No wonder they call you detective." Her lips lifted in a smile. "I already told you I acted on opportunity."

"In a way that was out of character." Max was as certain Toni wanted him as he was that she had a bad case of nerves.

"And you know this how?" She drummed her fingertips on the table, trying hard to maintain her nonchalant façade.

Max grinned. "Gut instinct."

Toni inclined her head. Not only did he understand her well but he seemed to see inside her, too. Her aggressive act was just that, but in no way did that minimize how badly she wanted this night.

He stopped her nervous tapping and

threaded his fingers through hers. "Relax, sweetheart."

The softly spoken endearment wrapped around her heart and her adrenaline picked up speed. "You really think that's possible?"

He shrugged. "I know so. We're going to get to know each other better. We'll have fun. And nothing will happen that you don't want to happen. So relax and come with me."

She'd follow him anywhere, Toni thought. And despite the fact that she'd never done anything that resembled a one-night stand before, she wanted *everything* to happen. She just needed to gather her nerve. Her hand entwined with his, she let him lead her around the bar and into a back room she hadn't seen earlier because of the crowds.

In the corner, beside the rack holding the pool cues, a Christmas tree took up a lot of space in the small room. The tree beckoned to her, with its worn ornaments, aged by time and handling, hanging from its branches. Though it wasn't professionally decorated with pricey ornaments like the one in the office, this Christmas display showed thoughtfulness, warmth, and caring.

She reached out and lightly fingered a cutout teddy bear hanging from a crudely bent pipe cleaner. "This is so sweet."

Max came up behind her. His body heat and

masculine scent put her nerve endings on high alert.

"Jake's daughter made it her first year in kindergarten," he said.

"And this one?" With a trembling hand, she pointed to a clay angel, made with obvious talent and love.

"A customer." Max's warm breath fanned her ear. "Jake could tell you who gave him each one."

Toni nodded, impressed. "And what was your contribution?"

"What makes you so sure I made one?"

"Intuition." The man would put his mark on everything in his life, she thought. Including herself.

"Smart woman. I supply the tree each year."

Toni turned to find him very close and what little composure remained nearly shattered beneath his steamy gaze.

"Ever play pool?" he asked, changing the subject.

Toni's shoulders lowered and she smiled, feeling on safer ground. "Too many times to count."

"Then we don't need lessons." He grabbed her hand and strode the few steps to the pool table. Wrapping his hands around her waist, he lifted her onto the lacquered edge.

She licked her lips, wondering why she'd deluded herself into an illusion of safety. Around Max, she was constantly off balance, desire never far away. "No lessons," she agreed, wondering what would come next.

"Then how about we play each other? For intriguing stakes." His deep eyes bored into hers.

"What do you have in mind?"

"It's called getting to know you. For every ball I miss, I admit something about myself. Something deep and personal or . . . something I desire." His voice deepened to a husky drawl.

She tried to swallow but her mouth had grown dry. "And if you get the ball into the pocket?"

She watched the pulse beat in his neck, and acting on impulse, she pressed a light kiss against his skin. He let out a low growl. "If I make my shot, you remove an article of clothing. Same rules apply for you. What do you say?"

Arousal beat a heavy rhythm in her veins. Naughty or nice, Toni thought. Did she have the nerve to participate in his game? To take their night to its ultimate conclusion?

Under ordinary circumstances, probably not. But nothing about Max or her growing feelings for him was typical—or easy. However, her pool game had never been a problem—not since she'd waitressed in college and learned from the best. "I say why not?"

He handed her a cue, then proceeded to set up the table. "Do you want to break or should I?"

"I'll do it." Toni figured it was a win-win situation. Either she revealed something about herself or he revealed a bare body part—either way *she* wouldn't be the one overexposed.

Max stepped back, leaning on his cue as Toni lined up her shot. The one thing he'd forgotten when suggesting this game was her skimpy outfit—and if the thought of their rules had him hot and bothered, the reality of watching her bent over the table inspired erotic images to rival his steamiest daydream.

"You do realize the lighter the stick the farther the follow-through," she said.

"It's also been said a heavier stick gives you more power," Max replied but he wasn't concentrating.

The white fur trim of her skirt had lifted a notch, revealing thigh-high stockings and an enticing glimpse of the pale skin peeking above the elastic lace trim. The sudden rise in heat owed nothing to room temperature and everything to his sexy elf. His fingers itched to cup her soft flesh and his body begged to be cradled in her feminine heat.

The sudden crack of the stick hitting the cue ball broke his train of thought and echoed in the otherwise silent room. Still in a sweat, Max forced himself to focus on the game in time to see a flash of color and a ball ease into the corner pocket. "I'm impressed."

She straightened and grinned, looking pleased with herself. "One lesson I learned early in life was to never agree to a game I couldn't win."

"I'll keep that in mind." He reached for the bottom of his shirt and yanked it over his head, grateful for her decent shot and the opportunity to cool off.

Her lashes fluttered quickly and her eyes opened wide as she stared at his bare chest.

"What's wrong? Did you forget the rules?" he asked.

She shook her head. "Of course not." Appearing more flustered than before, she settled in for the next round of play. But this time her hands shook and Max knew for sure his lack of clothing had rattled her. At least now they were on equal footing, he thought, taking in the seductive wiggle of her behind as she lined up her shot.

Sure enough, the next ball went shimmying toward the back wall, missing the pocket. "Sorry, sweetheart. Confession time."

She turned toward him, eyes big and imploring, a pout on her lips.

He shook his head. "No poor-me look is going to sway me, now spill." He paused, thinking of her alternatives. "Or you could always opt to speed the game along and remove an item of clothing."

"My sweet sixteen was my worst birthday," she said quickly, obviously making her choice.

He suppressed a laugh. "What happened?" He stepped closer, wishing she'd taken him up on his alternative offer.

"My dog ran away."

"I'm not buying that." He folded his arms across his chest, gratified when her eyes followed the movement. "But I am listening."

Her arm brushed his and she didn't break contact as she said, "My father died suddenly, the day before I turned sixteen."

Max breathed in deeply. A punch in the gut would have been more gentle, but it was his own fault. He'd suggested they reveal something deep and personal, and she had. She trusted him, showing it far more than if she'd removed her clothes.

"What happened?" he asked softly. Though she couldn't have any fond memories of the man, losing a parent couldn't be easy. "Heart attack?"

She nodded. "And instead of grief, I felt nothing but relief." The strain in her face and the guilt in her eyes were obvious. "And here I thought my shooting first would leave *you* more exposed." She shook her head and treated him to a brief smile. "Your turn." She gestured to the cue.

Max swallowed hard. Had he really thought this would be light and easy?

"Okay." Still shaken, he bent over the table and took in his options before lining up his shot, missing the pocket by too much.

He felt her light touch as she tapped him on the shoulder. He turned to find her in his personal space, within kissing distance. He reached for her shoulders and held on.

"You didn't have to do that," she whispered, calling him on his deliberately missed shot. An easier play had sat by the corner pocket but he'd chosen to forfeit instead.

"No, I didn't. But I wanted to." He'd had two choices. Open a vein and exchange information or watch her peel off the clingy green suit.

No matter how much he'd rather see her undress, he owed her and had to reveal a personal secret. She'd opened up to him tonight. Twice. If his goal was getting closer, he had to return the favor. Besides, he wanted to let her in. For the first time, he wanted to connect with a woman in more places than in bed. He'd proven himself adept at making selfish choices in life, Max thought, but not when it came to Toni. She was too special.

Gratitude flickered in her eyes and she waited in silence for him to pay up. He wasn't comfortable and hated like hell for having put himself in this position, but he supposed that spoke of Toni's effect on him. "My father resents me for leaving the business and I've never measured up to Stephan as Dad's favorite son." He tensed, having admitted his deepest vulnerability and laid it out there for her to see.

Her gaze softened. "Your father's a fool, and if you repeat a word of that to my boss, you'll pay in spades," she said, then wrapped her arms around his neck and pulled him closer.

Her lips lingered over his and as his chest rasped against her fur-lined V-neck, he needed more than a simple kiss. He fumbled for her zipper, the one that would allow him to peel off the outfit and bare her for him to see. But she pulled back before he could get a decent grasp and he groaned.

"Your last miss didn't count," she said in a husky voice. "Now play pool."

He wagged a finger in the air. "Like I said, naughty girl."

"What fun is it if you don't have to work for it?"

"Trust me, sweetheart, it'd be plenty fun. But if you insist, I'll take another turn." Having laid his soul bare, he knew it was time to turn up the heat. "But before I make this next shot . . ."

"You're too confident about your gaming abilities," she said, interrupting him.

"Aren't you the one who said never play a game you can't win? But if at any point you change your mind . . ."

She shook her head. "I wouldn't have let you drive all the way out here if I wasn't sure."

He let out a slow breath of air that did little to help his rapidly beating heart. "Just remember, it's your choice."

She looked at him in a way no one—no woman—had ever looked at him before, with just the right mixture of trust, reverence, and desire to make a man fall to his knees.

"You're a nice guy, Max."

He'd never been called nice before and he knew his actions tonight were as unique as she was. "You're pretty damn special yourself." He leaned over the table and easily made his next shot, then walked a few steps to line up the next. "But something tells me you won't be thinking such great thoughts about me after this," he said, sinking another ball as he spoke, then his third before shifting her way.

He focused on her and his breath caught in his throat. She'd left her shoes under the table in the other room and Max hadn't realized how little remained—the shirt, skirt, and belt, all three items she'd discarded while he was upping the ante and making his shots.

She faced him now, his most erotic dream come to life. Her clothes lay in a pile beside her.

Her black hair, tousled and full, caressed her shoulders. The body he'd glimpsed through the barrier of clothing and imagined in his mind had nothing on reality. A black lace bra cut in a deep V contrasted with and revealed creamy white mounds of flesh, while a whisper-light-looking bikini barely covered her feminine secrets.

She met his gaze and shrugged, a deep blush staining her cheeks and an embarrassed fidget to her stance. "I forgot to mention that when I lose—no matter how unlikely—I always pay up."

He edged his finger beneath one delicate bra strap, savoring the feel of her soft flesh beneath his roughened fingertips. "If you consider this a loss, then we have nothing further to—"

"Shh." She placed one finger over his lips. "That was a figure of speech."

His tongue darted out and he tasted her, a combination of salty skin and female softness. She sucked in a startled breath but she didn't remove her hand. Instead she traced the outline of his mouth with her fingertip, leaving him incredibly aroused by her touch.

"The game's over, Max, and I'd call it even."

He grinned. "Win–win."

"Mmm-hmm."

Taking that as his cue, Max did what he'd been dying to do since he'd laid eyes on her standing beside the Christmas tree—he spanned her bare waist with his hands, curling his fingers around her back and kneading his palms into her skin.

She let out a low, throaty moan. Need, want, and desire collided as her back arched and her breasts reached toward him, almost as if in supplication. Max didn't want to deny her.

And he could no longer deny himself.

Chapter 4

One night. Toni told herself she'd earned one night with this very special man. Then she could hang on to the memories and get on with her busy life. She refused to let herself dwell on what kind of emptiness that life would hold now that she'd known Max.

He'd settled her on the table and the lacquer felt cool against her hot, fevered skin, making her more aware of her surroundings and what was to come. She spread her thighs and he stepped inside, then bent his head and captured her nipple in his mouth, suckling her through the filmy black lace. His teeth grazed her flesh, then his tongue soothed and white-hot darts of need pulsed inside her. Her reaction was immediate, the pull starting at point of contact and causing intense contractions deep in her belly and down lower.

"You like that?"

Her answer came out a low, husky growl.

"Is that a yes?" He cradled her tender flesh in one hand and treated her other breast to the same lavish attention as the first.

She squirmed against the hard surface and slick moisture trickled between her legs as warmth and desire exploded inside her. "That's a yes."

He lifted his head and met her gaze. "You like to play."

"When it goes both ways." She raised her hands, placing both palms not just on his bare chest, but against his nipples.

Slowly, she raked her nails downward, watching, gratified, as his eyes glazed with heated emotion.

He groaned aloud. "You have no idea what you do to me."

"Oh, I think I can guess." Because she knew what *he* did to her. Every nerve ending came to life, raw and exposed, sizzling with live currents of desire.

"No need to guess when I can show you," he said, bringing his mouth down hard on hers. Frenzied, his kiss expressed an immediate need to be as close as possible.

His tongue swept inside the deep recesses of her mouth, mimicking the ultimate act. It wasn't a joining of bodies in the biblical sense, but another, just as intimate means of climbing toward satisfaction. His strong hands slid from her waist to her thighs and he grazed the tops of her stockings with his thumbs while his fingertips teased the outer edges of her panties. With his whisper-soft and erotically arousing movements, he let her know what he had in store.

And Toni wanted more. She arched her back and her hips jerked forward, reflexively, searching for his harder, deeper touch. He didn't deny her. He broke the kiss and concentrated on her need, cupping her feminine mound in his palm. The heat and weight of his hand against her barely covered flesh stirred long-dormant sensations and when he pushed aside the thin lace and dipped his fingers inside her moist, waiting heat, she thought she'd died and gone to heaven.

She was hot and aroused, on the brink of falling over a precipice, a tumble she had no desire to take alone. She leaned back to catch her breath, intending to make her desire known and she caught a glimpse of their position. She was barely dressed, her legs spread wide, with Max's lean body settled between them. She was open and vulnerable, physically as well as emotionally. The intimacy they were sharing struck her as strongly as her rampaging emotions. And when he leaned over, covering her body with his so he could rest his cheek against hers, he found a way closer to her heart.

She shut her eyes against the wave of emotion she wasn't ready to deal with and instead wrapped her legs around his waist in a provocative suggestion. "Make love to me, Max."

His deep blue eyes met hers. "Be sure, Toni." His breathing was as ragged as her emotions. "Because if we go any further there's no way I can stop."

She'd come into this night with seduction in mind and though everything had changed, including the man, there was no way she could walk away from him now. Still, he had to understand her behavior wasn't normally so wanton. She didn't know why it mattered so much, but it did.

She caressed his face with one hand. "I

wouldn't have asked you if I wasn't sure, but . . ."

He grabbed for her hand. "But what?"

"No matter how bold I've been tonight, I want you to know I don't usually sleep with a man I just met."

"I know."

"You do?"

He nodded. "Because I feel like I've known you all my life."

She felt the same but couldn't bring herself to admit the truth out loud. She licked her already moist lips. "There's something else you need to know." She couldn't think beyond now. Not that he'd asked but the emotional pull between them was too strong to ignore.

He shook his head. "Enough talking, don't you think?" To make his point, he slipped one finger back into her panties, parting her sensitive folds and moving his fingertip deeply inside her.

She closed her eyes and exhaled a soft moan as he encountered the desire he'd created inside her.

"So wet, so ready for me."

The man did have a point. "Talking can wait." She forced her heavy eyelids open. "So what did you have in mind?"

"I'm going to do what you asked, sweetheart. I'm going to make love to you. But I want you to do something for me first." He reached into his front pocket and pulled out the anklet she'd had on earlier in the evening.

She eyed the object with surprise.

"I took it from the car." He answered her unspoken question and shook the accessory in the air. The light chime of bells echoed in the silent bar. "Wear these for me."

Her heart beat out a rapid pulse and excitement tingled inside her. "Mind if I ask why?" she asked, curiously aroused by the suggestion.

"I want to hear bells when I come inside you," he said and his blue eyes flared with heat. "And every time you hear the ringing of chimes, I want you to think of me."

She never broke eye contact as she raised her leg and perched it on the edge of the table. With a nod of approval, he turned to his task, taking his time, rolling the stocking down her leg, inch by tantalizing inch. When he finished one, she propped her other leg so he could peel off another of her few remaining layers.

Then he snapped the anklet closed. "Perfect," he said, taking in her wanton pose.

With her legs spread wide, Toni ought to have been embarrassed, but all she felt was a keen sense of carnal anticipation. "Well, you've got me where you want me."

She shifted her leg, shaking her foot so he

could hear the light tinkling of bells. To her surprise, the sound turned from light and playful to highly erotic, charging the already electric atmosphere even further. "So what do you plan to do with me?"

With her help, he eased the last remaining undergarment off her legs, letting her panties fall to the floor. "I already told you. I'm going to make love to you." Then he knelt down, dipped his head, and proceeded to do just that, in a way she hadn't expected or anticipated. In a way much more intimate than she'd imagined.

His hot breath covered her feminine mound and his tongue delved deep into her core. Resting back on her elbows, she gave herself up to sensation, to the masterful strokes and fiery darting motions that had her hips gyrating and her body arching, beseeching him for more. He complied, bringing her higher, nearly to the brink of orgasm.

"Max!" She writhed beneath him, unable to express her desire further, not with her body tense and her climax so close. But she knew she didn't want her first time to be alone. Wonderful yet unfulfilling at the same time. He seemed to understand because his nuzzling caresses slowed and the waves subsided, leaving her empty.

Next thing she knew, she was being lifted and

carried in his arms. "We're going where?" she wondered aloud, her body protesting the very cessation of pleasure she'd asked for.

"Upstairs." Max made his way to the back door and up a dimly lit staircase. "Somehow, thoughts of our first time on a pool table don't work for me."

Not that he'd had the presence of mind to realize that before she'd called out his name, he thought. Prior to that moment, he'd have taken her on the hard surface without thought or reason, he'd been so far gone. Lost in her dewy essence.

"See? I told you you were a nice guy." Her arms snaked around his neck, her bare body crushed against his chest. "Now hurry."

He managed a laugh, barely able to make his way up the stairs, open his door, and hit the bedroom before lowering her to the bed and sealing his mouth to hers. But kissing wasn't enough for either of them and her hands fumbled with the snap on his jeans. Frustrated with the barrier between them, he rose to shuck his pants and briefs, and to dig protection from the back of his nightstand drawer, not an easy task in the dim room, lit only by the glow of light from the street lamp outside.

As he knelt over her, a wash of emotion swept through him, strong and tender, something he knew damn well he'd never felt before. He cupped her thighs, widening her legs, then slid his fingers over her damp flesh. He met her velvet gaze, watched as her eyes glazed at the same moment her hips rose in response to the slick strokes of his hand.

A soft purr escaped her throat, a sound of frustrated need.

"Just making sure you're ready for me, sweetheart."

"I am." She took him by surprise, managing to flip him to his side, switching their positions, her ending up on top. "I realize you're trying to be a gentleman our first time." Toni swung her leg over his until she straddled his thighs. "But there's no reason to wait."

"I like the way you think." And he more than liked her.

After making use of the condom he'd found earlier, he grasped her hips, fully participating as she lowered herself onto his hard erection. He gritted his teeth as heaven surrounded him and he entered her tight, moist heat.

She let out a shuddering sigh. "It's . . ." She bit down on her lower lip. "It's never been like this before." Awe and something more infused her voice, letting him know she felt not just the physical, but the emotional connection, as well.

Needing to touch her in other ways, he lifted his upper body to meet her lips in a too brief kiss before leaning back against the pillows.

She shifted slightly and his body shook with the restraint of holding back, of letting her mentally adjust to a connection he'd already recognized and accepted.

He reached up to unhook the clasp of her bra and she let the flimsy garment fall to the side, revealing twin mounds of rounded flesh. Her black hair fell over her shoulders, in stark contrast to her pale skin. He'd never seen a more incredible sight. His body swelled and hardened further while her muscles contracted to accommodate him, arousing him even more.

Max had said he felt as if he'd known her forever, and cocooned inside her, he knew he was right. His heart pounded as hard and fast as the adrenaline flowing through him. And then she began to move, beginning a rhythm he picked up immediately. Each circular motion built upon the already growing waves rocking his body. Every clench of her thighs ground their bodies more intimately and drove him that much deeper inside her. Fire licked at his skin and waves of desire pushed him higher, and from the soft cries escaping her lips, he knew she felt it, too.

Carnal sensation mixed with a basic awareness. He'd had sex before, but Toni was right. They were making love.

He glided inside, her tight, slick passage accepting him, taking him with her just as her frenzied movements carried her up and over the edge.

"Max." She cried out his name, her body pulsing around his, beckoning him to follow. And as his climax hit, engulfing him in sensation, Max heard the ringing of bells.

Toni curled her legs beneath her and poked around in the candy dish he'd brought from his small kitchen. She clenched her thighs together and the waves of awareness hit her once more. How could she still be so sensitive and aroused?

She glanced over at Max through hooded eyes. He watched her intently, not saying a word. What was there to say? What they'd just shared defied description. Though she knew she'd clammed up on him afterward, her thoughts were in turmoil. She'd planned a seduction she could walk away from, not a relationship that would be hard to let go of. But no matter how she tried to tell herself she barely knew him, he'd not only touched her body, he'd touched her heart.

"Do you always work up such an appetite?" He rested his arm across the pillows, skimming his fingertips along her shoulders.

"I already told you I don't do this often, so how do you expect me to answer that?" She knew she'd snapped and held up her hands in apology. "I don't know what's wrong with me."

"I do."

He gently took the bowl out of her hands and placed it on the nightstand. "It was intense and it scared you."

She narrowed her gaze, not sure if she liked how well he read her. "If that's the case then how come you're so calm and composed?"

He took her hand, his thumb tracing slow circles into her palm, and her stomach curled with warmth. "I'm a jaded guy who's been around?" he said lightly.

Toni sensed more beneath his words but she couldn't tell if she was projecting her hopes and dreams into his unspoken words.

"And if I'm not thrown, I think the more important question is how come you *are*?" he asked.

She bit down on her lower lip. She couldn't very well tell him she'd slept with him wanting only one night. For one thing it was callous, and regardless of what he wanted from her, she had no desire to hurt him. And for another, what she'd wanted going into this night was no longer what she desired now.

Now she wanted a chance to see where things with Max could lead, but the thought frightened her beyond reason. After all, what did she know of long-term, stable relationships? Of depending on another person when she only knew how to depend on herself? Most of all, she feared losing her independence to a man and what it could cost her.

But she wanted to learn about sharing and caring, and she wanted to see that being in a relationship didn't mean losing the autonomy she cherished. She wanted to learn all those things.

With Max.

"Let's say you're right." She forced herself to meet his compassionate and oh-so-sexy gaze. "And let's say what's between us is passionate and . . ."

"Intense." He treated her to his most charming grin.

Then again, any grin she'd seen from him was appealing and her heart twisted with emotion. "Okay, intense. It's been one night. What exactly are you proposing we do about it?" she asked and her heart clenched with possibilities.

In response, he pulled her into his arms and toppled her to the mattress, sandwiching her body between his and the bed. "I suggest we go with the flow and see where things lead."

And if his hard erection against her stomach was any indication, she knew exactly where they were headed. At least for now. "You do know how to tempt me." And going with the flow wasn't a high-pressure situation.

In fact, it was one she couldn't wait to handle. She reached down and grasped his hard erection in her hands. He exhaled and a masculine groan reverberated from his body through hers.

He somehow managed a harsh laugh. "Tempting you is a pleasure." He brushed a sweet kiss across her lips. "Then I have one day at a time to show you we can be as good out of bed as in."

His hips jerked forward, brushing against her thigh. Heat rocked her and arousal began a steady pulsing rhythm.

Toni closed her eyes. Easier to concentrate on the physical than on the emotional, she thought, letting sensation take over. He had only to let his desire be known and her body came alive.

"Look at me."

She opened her eyes but she wasn't able to meet his gaze.

"I'm not going to let you hide from me." He cupped her cheek in his hand but didn't turn her head for her.

The tender gesture brought an unnerving lump to her throat. Not only did he understand her so well but he cared, too. What they'd found in one night was rare and special and she sensed he felt it, too.

She fought the inclination to flee and met his

patient gaze. "I don't want to hide from you." Her words came out a whisper and she realized she meant it. Reservations be damned.

"Then don't." Max pulled the covers back, revealing their bare bodies to the cooler air, then reached over and turned on a bedside lamp. He wanted her trust, wanted no secrets, no clothing, not even darkness between them. Physical intimacy was the only way he knew how to start.

The rest would have to come. They'd already made love once, and when they did again, there'd be no hiding.

For either of them.

He caressed her body with his gaze, following the slender lines and full curves, appreciation and more settling inside him. Then he watched as she did the same. She took in his body, her eyes widening as they traveled from his face, down to the erection he couldn't hide.

"What do you want from me?" she asked softly, but he had a hunch she already knew because as she spoke, she slid backward, settling into the pillows behind her.

Her black hair fanned across the ivory sheets. *His* sheets. A primitive urge to possess her, to make her his again—this time forever—took hold. "I want everything, sweetheart. But I'll take as much as you're willing to give."

He inched forward, making his way toward

her. Her eyes lit with excitement and desire, diluted by an apprehension only his time and trust could overcome.

She surprised him by extending her arms. "I want to make love to you, Max. Lights on, nothing hidden."

Her vulnerability hit him hard where it counted most—his heart.

Toni awoke feeling decadent and relaxed after falling asleep without trouble for the first time in ages. Of course her late-night activity could have had something to do with that. So could her . . . lover.

Lover. She tested the word on her tongue, realizing it was too generic, too detached and indifferent, to describe their encounter. Whatever sexual relationships she'd had in the past, no one had made it past the walls she'd built up since she'd been a child. How could any man have gotten inside her when she'd feared emotional closeness would result in unhealthy dependence? But Max had not only found her heart, she'd willingly let him in.

"Max?" She sat up in bed, realizing she was alone.

Noise from the shower in the bathroom alerted her to his location. She was in Max's bedroom while he showered for the day. Soon he'd come out—would he wrap a towel around his neck? His waist? Neither? Curling her legs beneath her, she forced deep breaths into her lungs. Whatever sharing a morning together entailed, it couldn't be any more intimate than the night they'd just spent.

And it wasn't reason for panic, she told herself, until the waves of anxiety began to ease. The man wasn't asking her for anything more than she was willing to give, and a nurturing, caring relationship would be a wonderful start to both the holiday season and a brand-new year.

The ringing of the telephone startled her and the answering machine picked up soon after. "Hi, Max." Toni recognized Stephan's voice. "Dad tells me you'll be running the new office. Since Santa's helper will be your assistant, it won't be too much of a strain," he said, a wry sound to his voice. "You owe me one. Later, big brother."

No sooner had Stephan's voice clicked off than Toni tossed the covers off, adrenaline flowing fast in her veins. Or maybe she was feeling a full-blown anxiety attack coming on. Was this fate's version of a joke? Or was she being punished for her descent into the world of the less repressed?

Where were her clothes? She glanced around the room, desperate to find something to put on. She'd finally found a man she could relate to, a man she desired, a man she trusted enough to let down her guard with.

And he'd be her new boss. A man she'd slept with the first night they'd met. A man who was now in control of her job—the symbol of the very independence she cherished. One-night stand or full-blown affair, it didn't matter. Because office romances never worked out, and when they fell apart, who was the one gone? Not the boss, but the co-worker. Office-wrecker.

She'd be out on her ear, no job, no references, no money—her blessed independence shot to hell, all because she'd fallen for the wrong man. "Where are my clothes?" she wailed aloud.

Downstairs. Scattered around the poolroom. She rolled her eyes, realizing her life had taken on surreal proportions. Her gaze fell to a pile of clothes on the chair which obviously substituted for a laundry hamper or a closet. She grabbed a sweatshirt and then turned to the desk and pilfered a sheet of paper.

"Dear Max," she wrote, feeling as if it were like "Dear John" and hating herself for it. She finished her letter, hoping what she said would be enough to save, if not her job, then at least a letter of recommendation for a position at a new firm. Starting over, Toni thought. Like her mother had each time she'd tried to make a stand and failed.

Her stomach clenching, she bolted for the door without looking back.

Chapter 5

Max looped a towel around his neck and headed out of the bathroom. He had to be at his parents' house early but damned if he'd miss one minute of time he could spend with Toni—who, he realized, was nowhere to be found.

Max glanced around but all he saw was a rumpled bed. "Son of a bitch." He muttered more under his breath.

He didn't need to look around his small apartment. Every instinct he had and prided himself on told him she was gone. What he didn't know was why.

He ran a frustrated hand through his hair. Yes he did. He knew exactly why she'd bolted. Fear, pure and simple. Because Max Corbin, ace detective, had made a major miscalculation when dealing with a vulnerable, skittish woman. Despite her calculated seduction, he didn't kid himself that Toni was anything less than vulnerable. That innocence was what held him in thrall. Her beauty would never fade but her looks weren't what had caused him to fall so damn hard. It was the whole package.

And Max had blown it. He'd tread lightly when he should have hit harder. He'd kept his feelings to himself, afraid of frightening her after one night. Maybe if he'd let her know he was certain they had long-term written all over them, she'd still be in his bed and not on her way back to New York City.

"Damn." Curses and regrets were the only things he could manage about now. He walked to the bed they'd shared and lowered himself onto the mattress. The sheets had cooled but his body hadn't. Not even a cold shower could dull the aching need she inspired.

He glanced at the clock but a folded note blocked his view of the numbers and his stomach plummeted as he read her hastily scrawled words. "Dear Max, Please remember I don't normally sleep with men I don't know. And don't hold last night against me. Toni."

Confusion mingled with a deep pain in his gut as he realized what she must have felt on waking up alone. Another reason to kick himself in the ass, Max thought. He should have let his family wait, and would have if not for his father's frail health.

Another choice curse rose to his throat but he stifled it, knowing it would do no good. He just needed to find Toni. He crumpled the note and tossed it to the nightstand, noticing his blinking answering machine for the first time. He wondered who'd called so early and hit play.

Listening to his brother's message provided not only insight into Toni's run but another reason to kick himself hard. Only Max would understand the sarcasm in the message and the fact that his brother was giving him a heads-up before his meeting with the old man. Only Max and Stephan realized he had no intention of returning to Corbin and Sons. But Toni, to whom he'd admitted his biggest failing and disappointment, might well believe he'd want to make his sick father happy.

She obviously thought she'd slept with her

boss. For a woman who needed security as much as other people needed air to breathe, that had to have been one hell of a slap in the face.

Max pulled on his jeans and made his way down to the empty bar. The pool table was just as they'd left it last night, but Toni had retrieved her clothing. Not a trace of her remained except in Max's heart.

Max entered his brother's luxury condo, an apartment opposite in furnishing and feel from Max's own casual over-the-bar rental.

"So what brings you to my neck of the woods?" Stephan asked, gesturing to a chair in the kitchen.

Max shook his head. He didn't have time to sit. Still, his brother had asked a fair question since Max couldn't remember the last time he'd shown up here unannounced. But today was different, just as his relationship with his twin had undergone a subtle shift since last night. Many things had changed since last night, he thought wryly.

Including his priorities. Max had driven into the city, postponing his meeting with his father in favor of finding Toni. Unfortunately, he had no idea where to begin, so he'd landed on his brother's doorstep first. Swallowing both his pride and his rule against talking about the women he slept with, Max unloaded on his brother. It was the first time in too damn long he'd had a heart-to-heart with his twin. Realizing how much he missed it and seeing the same in Stephan's face, Max knew the distance had closed.

Distance Max had placed there for no good reason. Just as Toni's insecurities drove her to succeed and to bolt this morning, Max now knew his own insecurities had driven him from his family. He planned to rectify both his and Toni's misperceptions—immediately.

Max finished relating last night's history to his brother.

Stephan nodded, while shaking his head at the same time. "I'm glad to see you screw up every once in a while. Makes the rest of us feel like you're human, too."

"Come again?" Max raised an eyebrow. "I screw up more than once in a while. Isn't that what Dad always says?"

"Dad says it to instill guilt and you buy into it every time. But you always hold your ground and live your life. To me that's not screwing up, that's playing it smart. A part of me has always envied that."

Shock rendered Max mute. For twins, he and his brother had been operating on opposite wavelengths for too long. "You don't want to be a lawyer?" Max asked.

"I never gave it a thought. It was expected and I followed through. Now it's all I know and I can't imagine doing anything else. But sometimes I wonder 'what if.'" He shrugged. "Then I take a look at how following a different road has kept you far from the family and I figure I'll accept my life as it is. But in case you're wondering, distancing yourself is the only screwup I think you've made." His brother let out a wry laugh. "Until now."

"Now meaning Toni." Just saying her name caused the twisting in Max's gut to return. He had the rest of his life to process his brother's admission and make things right. He had too little time to catch Toni and explain before she withdrew for good. "I need her address."

"There's no point." Stephan pushed off the wall and headed for the mugs in the cabinet. "Coffee?"

"No, thanks, and why the hell not?"

"She's not at home. I stopped by the office to pick up a file and she was there sorting through boxes." Stephan laughed. "Damn but you need to calm down."

"After I talk to her."

His brother eyed him in surprise. "This is a hell of a lot more than a one-night stand, isn't it?"

Max clenched and unclenched his fists. "It'd better be or I'm looking at a lousy Christmas and a miserable New Year."

"Well, I'll be damned. I wonder what I missed in her."

"Too late for you to find out now," Max said in warning, turned, and started for the door before spinning back to face his brother. "Hey, Stephan, I owe you one for the heads-up on what the old man wanted."

His twin shrugged. "I figured since you showed up last night, it was the least I could do."

Max laughed. Showing up had brought Toni into his life. "Then it looks like I owe you double. See ya later." Max opened the door and stepped into the hall.

"Don't think for one minute that I won't cash in," Stephan called as Max slammed the door shut behind him.

Toni needed to keep busy or else she'd think and she could not afford to think. Not about last night and how much she'd enjoyed herself, not about Max and how much she'd grown to like and care for him, and certainly not about the fact that she'd slept with her new boss. What irony. After years of avoiding the situation with Stephan, she'd stepped right into it with his twin.

She let out a slow breath of air. Okay, apparently she couldn't avoid thinking but maybe she could drown out the sound of her own thoughts. She flipped on the radio in her near-empty office. As expected, Christmas music filled the air. She tried humming and when that didn't work she sealed the last box, while singing out loud, but no way could she escape the fact that she'd fallen in love with Max Corbin.

Fallen in love. She shook her head, unable to believe the truth. She was a woman who hadn't grown up watching a loving relationship and who'd never once deluded herself that happily ever after was in her future. Yet in one meeting, over the course of one night—one glorious night—she'd fallen in love. And all the security she'd worked for, all the independence she'd strived for, now hung in the balance.

Her heart beat out a rapid cadence, panic and other undefinable emotions parading inside her while the music mocked her thoughts. No merry Christmas, no happy New Year for her this year. She closed her eyes, singing the final verse along with the song. "We wish you a merry Christmas, we wish you a merry Christmas, we wish you a merry Christmas . . . and you're out on your ear." Toni added her own ending to the well-known tune.

"Is that really what you think of me?"

Startled, Toni whirled around to find herself face-to-face with Max. Leaning against her doorframe, he was the epitome of her fantasy come to life. And to think, she hadn't known she had any. "Hello, Max."

He inclined his head. "Toni."

She attempted to swallow but her mouth was too dry. "What are you doing here?"

"I wanted to get a few things straight." He walked into her office, making the small area even smaller by virtue of his overwhelming presence.

She grasped the cardboard edges of the box. "I can tender my resignation if it would make things easier." She spoke without meeting his gaze.

She heard him exhale hard. "Again, is that what you think of me? Do you really believe I'd have taken you home and made love to you, knowing I was your boss, and then demanded your job the next day?"

Toni wondered if she imagined the hurt in his voice. She shook her head. "Truthfully, I haven't thought things through."

"No, you're just feeling, aren't you?" His voice softened. "Acting on instinct and fear."

"What do you expect, Max? I woke up to

find out I had slept with my soon-to-be-boss. Whose job is on the line now? Yours or mine?"

"No one's, I hope." He eased himself onto the edge of her desk, too close for her peace of mind.

So close she could inhale his masculine scent and arousal hit her all over again, but he wasn't asking permission and she wasn't in a position to argue. "So you're suggesting we put last night behind us and work together?" She tried to laugh but the sound was harsh and she didn't mean it anyway.

If he could work side by side with her, after what they'd shared, she'd misjudged him. Yet even before she met his serious and compelling gaze, she knew better. How could she not? She'd accepted him into her body, felt him hard and hot inside her, giving as much as he got in return.

Then there were the emotional revelations, Toni thought. Men didn't open up and share unless they cared. But she was still at a loss.

"I'm not suggesting we work together, either. I told you last night I do my own thing. And yes, my father's disappointed, and no, he's not finished trying to convince me to return. But he's been unsuccessful in the past and he'll continue to be unsuccessful in the future. Law isn't what I want. I am *not* going to be your boss."

She glanced down and saw her hands were shaking. "But Stephan said . . ."

"Stephan was giving me advance warning about what to expect at my meeting with Dad. You heard what Dad wants, not what will be." He touched her cheek, his hand strong and gentle. "But that's not the real issue, is it?"

She forced herself to meet his gaze. "If you know so much, then tell me what is."

"I'm not your boss. I'm just a man who's desperately in love with you. So the issue is, are you going to run from your feelings because of your past? Or are you going to stay and face them . . . and give us a chance?"

In that instant, Toni's past and present flashed in front of her eyes, a kaleidoscope of memories, some good, some bad, some satisfying, but way too many lonely ones. Lonely by choice not necessity, she thought. Last night she'd chosen Max and last night she hadn't felt alone or isolated.

She was a woman who'd always prided herself on her ability to stand on her own two feet, yet she wanted nothing more than to throw herself into his arms.

"So what are you waiting for?" he asked.

She blinked, refocusing on her surroundings. On Max. "Did I speak out loud?"

He watched her intently. "No, I'm just a mind reader."

Her mind was jumbled, her heart racing, and his earlier words came back to her. "What did you say?"

"I'm just a mind reader."

"Before that."

"I'm not your boss," he said.

"In between those two things."

"I'm a man desperately in love with you?" He grinned.

His devastating smile nearly knocked her off her feet and a sparkle twinkled in his blue eyes. A weight she hadn't been aware of carrying her whole life eased and lifted inside her.

She could run and hide or give the future a chance. No contest, Toni thought, a smile pulling at her lips.

"I asked what you're waiting for?" His voice was gruff with emotion, his once-certain smile faltering as his insecurity became obvious.

More than anything else, his ability to own up to his feelings and emotions touched her heart. She could free hers and learn from him. Be independent and still be in love.

If she dared.

His gaze locked with hers. He lifted his hand, revealing a green sprig of mistletoe and holding it up high. "I thought we could try it again." He extended his free hand, holding it out to her. "Get it right this time."

Toni rushed into his arms and Max lowered

his head for a kiss that felt too long in coming. He'd never admit it out loud but she'd had him sweating there for a minute. But now she was his.

Her lips were soft and willing, welcoming him. His hands slipped around her waist beneath the band of her sweatshirt until he encountered soft skin. She let out a faint sigh and leaned back against the desk, letting his body mesh with hers. Her thighs spread and his groin settled hard against her stomach.

But warning bells went off in his head. "Not again, sweetheart. Not until we've got a few things settled."

"Mmm." She purred in his ear and her hand slipped to the bulge in his jeans.

Max nearly caved right then, but knowing his future was on the line, he forced himself to pull back. He'd messed up once and she'd run at the first opportunity. He wasn't about to screw up again. "I love you" was saying a hell of a lot for a man who'd always lived alone—but it wasn't a declaration of future intent. And a woman like Toni both deserved and needed one.

And for the first time, Max realized, so did he. "Toni."

She met his gaze.

"I don't usually sleep with women I just met."

She grinned. "That's good because I feel as if I've known you all my life."

"Then prove it. I'm a slob. I don't put my clean clothes away, I wear them straight from a pile on the chair. I squeeze the toothpaste from the middle, I drink milk out of the carton, and those are the positives." He paused, deadly serious. "But I still think we have a chance."

Her eyes were misty and damp but her smile never dimmed. "I've been known to hang stockings from doorknobs and eat Chinese food out of the carton. For breakfast." She smoothed one hand down his thigh, the other hand never leaving its strategic position on his groin.

His body protested his prolonged wait in making her his but his mind and heart knew he was doing it right this time. "I go to sleep too late and wake up too early. But I promise to give you the best that I've got to make us work. You can trust me and you never have to fear me—" Max never got to finish.

She covered his mouth with hers in the sweetest, hottest, most honest kiss he'd ever known. He paused only to slam her door closed and undress her, dropping his jeans as quickly as possible. He entered her quickly, this time on the desk she'd be leaving behind. When the aftershocks subsided, his body was still deep inside hers.

"This was naughty," she murmured.

"I thought that was your plan."

She laughed. "Only with you, Max. You bring out my decadent side."

"My pleasure, sweetheart. It's something I plan on doing again." His groin began to harden once more, and Max proceeded to seal their bodies, just as they'd sealed their future. Being naughty under the mistletoe.

Read on for an excerpt from
DON'T LOOK DOWN

by Jennifer Crusie and Bob Mayer

Available in hardcover from
St. Martin's Press

Lucy Armstrong was standing on the Eugene Talmadge Memorial Bridge when she first spotted the black helicopter coming at her through the sunset.

Based on the rest of her day, that wasn't going to be good.

Twenty feet to her right, her assistant director, Gleason Bloom, ignored the chopper and worked the set like a depraved grasshopper, trying to organize what Lucy had already recognized as her career's most apathetic movie crew. Her gratitude to Gloom for his usual good work was only exceeded by her gratitude that he hadn't yet seen that the movie's stunt coordinator was Connor Nash, now half hidden behind his black stunt van, arguing with a sulky-looking brunette.

Of course, Gloom was bound to notice Connor sooner or later. *I'll just point out that it's only four days,* she thought. *Four lousy days for really good money, we check on Daisy and Pepper, we finish up somebody else's movie, we go home, no harm, no foul—*

Off to the west, the helicopter grew closer, flying very low, just above the winding Savannah River. All around were brush and trees, garnished with swamp and probably full of predators. "The low country," Connor had called it, as if that were a good thing instead of a euphemism for "soggy with a chance of alligator." And now a helicopter—

Lucy rocked back as fifty-some pounds of five-year-old niece smacked into her legs at top speed, knocking her off balance and almost off her feet.

"Aunt Lucy!"

"Pepper!" She went down to her knees, inhaling the Pepper smell of Twizzlers and Fritos and Johnson's baby shampoo as she hugged the little girl to her, trying to avoid the binoculars slung around Pepper's neck. "I am *so glad* to see you!" she said, rocking her back and forth.

Pepper pulled back, her blond Dutch Boy haircut swinging back from her round, beaming face. "We will have *such* a good time now that you're here. We will play Barbies and watch videos, and I will tell you about my Animal of the Month, and we will have a party!" Her plain little face was lit with ecstasy. "It will be so, so good!" She threw her arms around Lucy's neck again and strangled her with another hug, smashing the binoculars into Lucy's collarbone.

"Yes," Lucy said, trying to breathe and hug back, thinking, *Great, now I have to play with Barbies*. She pulled back to get some air and said, "Nice binoculars!" as she tried to keep from getting smacked with them again.

"Connor gave them to me," Pepper said. "I can see *everything* with them."

"Good for Connor." Over Pepper's head Lucy saw the helicopter cut across a bend in the river, zipping through an impossibly small opening between two looming oak trees. *It's heading right for us,* she thought, *and whoever is flying that thing is crazy*. Then Connor raised his voice and said, *"No,"* and she looked over to see the young brunette step up into his face, giving as nasty as she got.

Lucy thought, *Good for you, honey,* and stood up, smiling at Pepper. "But I have to work first, so—"

"I will help you work," Pepper said, clinging to her, her smile turning tense. "I will be your assistant and bring you apples and water."

Lucy nodded. "You will be a *huge* help." She took the little girl's hand and looked back at Connor. After kicking herself twelve years ago for having been so stupid as to marry him, looking at those broad shoulders and slim hips now reminded her why her brain had gone south when she was twenty-two. *Good thing I'm smarter now,* she thought, and looked again.

The way he was talking to the brunette, the way she leaned into his comfort zone, they were sleeping together. And she looked to be about twenty-two.

That must be his target age, she thought. *I should tell Gloom that, he'll laugh.*

Gloom. She looked back toward the set and didn't see him, but the helicopter was now zipping underneath one of the port cranes, then banking hard toward the bridge. Lucy shook her head, trying not to be impressed. The pilot probably had *Top Gun* in permanent rotation on his DVD player. *Whatever happened to the strong, silent type?*

"Aunt Lucy?" Pepper said, her smile gone, her face much too worried for a five-year-old.

"You'll be a *huge* help," Lucy said hastily. "*Huge*. Now, where is your mama—*Ouch!*"

Her head snapped back as Gloom yanked on her long black braid from behind. "*Connor Nash,*" he said, and she dropped Pepper's hand and grabbed the base of her braid to take the pressure off her skull.

"Yeah." Lucy tried to pry her braid out of his hand. "I was going to mention that."

"Really? *When*?"

"As late in the game as possible. Which appears to be now."

"What were you *thinking*?" Gloom glared at her, his gawky form looming beside her.

"Gloom?" Pepper said, and he looked down and let go of Lucy's braid.

"Peppermint!" He picked her up, swooshing her up to hug her, almost getting beaned by her binoculars as he smacked a kiss on her cheek.

Pepper giggled, happy again, and wrapped her arms around his neck.

"I'm *so glad* you're here," she said, strangling him. "We will have a party."

"You bet." Gloom peeled one of her arms away from his windpipe. "Tell you what, go get your mama and tell her we need to make plans. There will have to be a cake—"

"*Yes!*" Pepper said, and tried to wriggle her

way to the ground. Gloom set her down, and she was off like a shot, blond hair flying and binoculars bouncing as she headed for the craft services table set up near Connor's van, the source of apples and candy and water bottles and, evidently, her mother.

Lucy frowned up at the sky. "We didn't order a helicopter today, did we?"

Gloom yanked her braid again.

"*Ouch. Stop* that."

"Now about that Aussie bastard," Gloom said.

Down the bridge, Connor looked up at them, distracted by the commotion, and saw Lucy for the first time. His face lit up—*God, he's beautiful,* she thought—and then he started up the bridge to her.

"Connor called and offered us an obscene amount of money to finish this thing and I said no," Lucy said, talking fast so that Gloom wouldn't say, "Hello, dickhead," when Connor reached them.

The brunette went after Connor, catching his arm, and he stopped and tried to shake her off.

Gloom's dark brows met over his nose. "If you said, no, why—"

"And then Daisy called and said to please come down because we hadn't seen her and Pepper in so long, and I said no, I'd send her the money to come visit us. . . ."

The brunette held on, but Connor yanked free, making her stumble back as he came up the bridge, oblivious to the chopper closing in on them. He kept his eyes on Lucy, everything in him focused completely on his objective.

And that's why I married you, Lucy thought.

"So why are we here?" Gloom said.

"Because Daisy put Pepper on the phone and I told her we weren't coming and she cried." Lucy switched her attention back to Gloom. "Pepper's not a crier, you know that, Gloom, but I understand that you hate Connor, so you go tell Pepper we're not staying. Take Kleenex. Meanwhile, I'll explain to Connor why he'll be directing these last four days himself instead of paying us a small fortune to do what we can do in our sleep."

"What?" Gloom said and turned to follow her eyes and saw Connor. "Oh, fuck."

"Be nice," Lucy said. "He—"

She broke off as the bubble-shaped helicopter suddenly gained altitude and swooped over the closest bridge tower, sharp against the red sun. Connor stopped and looked up at it and then got an odd look on his face, anger or surprise, she couldn't tell.

Gloom stepped closer to her as the chopper dived to the middle of the bridge and abruptly slowed, coming to a perfect hover just to the east, well out of the way of the cables that lined the roadway. Then it pirouetted smoothly, moved sideways down the bridge, and to the ground. Pepper came running back from craft services to say, "*Wow,*" as the chopper touched down lightly next to the roadway.

"There's no helicopter on the shooting schedule," Gloom said, frowning. "And that one has—is that a machine gun?"

Lucy peered at the ugly-looking contraption bolted to the right skid. "I think so." She bent to pick up Pepper. "I don't think it's on Connor's schedule either. Look at him."

Connor's shoulders were set as he reversed direction and headed for the chopper, walking past the brunette without even acknowledging she was there until she grabbed his arm again. *Honey, never interrupt him when he's on a mission,* Lucy thought and looked back at the helicopter.

A man got out, ignoring the blades whooping by just over his head, broad shouldered and slim hipped in Army camouflage, with none of Connor's electricity or glossy good looks, just tan and solid in the middle of the noise and wind. He walked forward out of rotor range and halted to look back at the chopper, his lantern jaw in profile, completely still in the storm, and Lucy lost her breath.

"Tell me that's my action star," she said.

Another man dressed in jeans, a black T-shirt, and flip-flops got out of the copter on the other side, tripping over the skid as he stumbled out from under the blades. Then he stood up and joined the quiet man on the edge of the road, swaggering as he went.

"*That's* your star," Gloom said. "Bryce McKay. Medium-famous comedian. Great at pratfalls. Action? Not so much."

"Right," Lucy said, but her eyes went back to the quiet man, so much like Bryce physically, so much his opposite in every other way. Anybody that still had to have his act together. None of that macho garbage that had driven her away from Connor after six months of marriage.

Connor shook off the brunette and moved down the bridge to the helicopter, his focus on the newcomer, his hands out at his sides. *Hell,* Lucy thought. *He's already gunning for this guy.*

The quiet man turned to face him. Connor stiffened, and the other man stared back, not moving.

"Oh, boy," Gloom said happily.

"Oh, great," Lucy said. "And they're both thinking, 'Mine's bigger than yours.'"

"I *love* this," Gloom said. "It's like *High Noon*. Maybe somebody will finally outdraw that son of a bitch."

"Yeah, that would be good except this is real life, not a Western," Lucy said, exasperated. "Why don't they just pull them out and show them to each other?"

"Pull out what?" Pepper said.

"Their binoculars." Lucy put the little girl down. "I have to go see what's going on, baby. You wait here with Gloom."

"I want to come," Pepper said, her smile gone.

"Oh, I do, too." Gloom picked up Pepper. "I think this is going to be *my* party."

"Try to control your joy," Lucy said and headed down the bridge to contain the disaster, trying not to admire the quiet man for remaining so still in the midst of the chaos.

Read on for a sneak peek at the thrilling

new romance from Lori Foster

CAUSING HAVOC

Coming soon from Berkley

Standing at the interior balcony, her bare arms folded over the cool steel railing, Eve Lavon watched the line dancing below. In so many ways, Roger's place was the perfect setting for a bachelorette party. The low-key honky-tonk offered drinks, dancing, private rooms, a festive environment . . . but God, she detested Roger. She didn't want to do business with the swine.

Blindly, Eve reached for her longneck beer sitting on the tiny round table beside her. She finished it off, then turned to head for the bar to get another.

The sight of a tall man, roughed up and rugged, standing in the doorway, stopped her in her tracks.

He perused the area with a jaundiced eye, lip curled in disgust, body set in lines of weariness. Obviously, Roger's place wasn't quite what he'd expected.

From the outside, Roger's Rodeo looked like any other small-time bar. From the inside, it boasted a disco atmosphere with an open first floor that overlooked the basement below by way of a balcony that circled the entire floor. Both levels provided a bar, and each floor had a smattering of private rooms. But the action happened downstairs: line dancing, mechanical bull rides, billiards, pinball machines.

Two-seater tables lined the balcony, with enough space between to accommodate spectators. Tonight, Eve had come to watch, to make a decision on whether or not to organize an event in one of the private rooms in the basement. Harmony, Kentucky, didn't have a lot of options, and most of what it did have, Roger owned. The group hiring her wasn't interested in going out of town, so . . .

The hunk locked eyes with her.

Eve's heart skipped a beat. It seemed her all-business night was about to include pleasure.

As he started forward, he looked . . . way too intense. And really beat-up. But sexy, too. Rock-hard and ripped, all machismo and confidence despite the bruises.

To Eve's surprise, when he got right in front of her, his mouth lifted on one side—and he stepped around her to peer over the balcony.

Playing hard to get? Amusement and interest unfurled inside her. Turning, Eve took up her position against the railing again. "First time here?"

Without taking his gaze from the dancers below, he rumbled, "Probably my last, too."

Nice, deep voice. A flutter stirred in her belly. "Not if you plan to be in Harmony long. Roger's Rodeo is about the only decent place to drink socially."

One thick shoulder lifted. "Drinking alone has its perks."

"Those being?"

"Less noise." He turned toward her, and his gaze boldly searched every inch of her person. "You drinking alone tonight?"

"Not anymore." She saluted him with her empty beer. "So did a bull stomp all over you, or did you forget your parachute when you jumped from the plane?"

He stared at her mouth. "It was a Russian bull, and mean as hell."

"I take it the bull won?"

"Actually, no."

"Ah. Well, looks are deceiving."

His gaze came back to hers. "I hope not."

Those three words dripped sensual suggestion. Eve almost sighed. How could one man possess so much appeal? It had been a very long time since she'd felt this drawn. She wanted to get closer to him. She wanted to touch him.

Even in the crowded bar, with the smell of liquor and sweat hanging in the air, she could detect his scent. Rich and reminiscent of the outdoors, it suggested that he'd had a long drive, probably with the windows down. She liked that.

His mussed, light-brown hair nearly matched the mellow color of his expressive eyes. He stood easily six-four, towering over her by damn near a foot. His worn jeans and black T-shirt hung loosely on his frame, but solid muscles showed anyway. Whatever he did, he kept his body shredded, without a single ounce of fat.

Eve glanced behind her, saw an empty nook, and said, "Wanna grab a seat?"

His gaze searched hers. "Is a seat my only option for now?"

Lord help her, she wanted to melt. Instead, she donned a cocky smile. "For now."

Both sides of his mouth lifted. "Then yeah, I'll take a seat, especially if it comes with a beer."

Finally having a good excuse, Eve wrapped her fingers around his wrist on the pretense of guiding him to the room. He had thick bones, hot skin, and crisp hair. The fact that her fingers couldn't completely encircle his wrist got her heart pumping double-time.

Along the way to the semi-private alcove, Eve paused at the bar to say, "Bring us some beers, will ya, Dave?"

"Be right there."

"Thanks." They reached the room just in time to head off another couple. "Sorry," Eve said, and slipped in before them.

Once inside, she had to release him, but she held out her hand. "I'm Eve Lavon, by the way."

He looked at her outstretched hand, but didn't accept the handshake. Instead, he captured her wrist, lifted her palm to his mouth, and put the gentlest of kisses there. Still holding on to her, he whispered, "Hi, Eve."

Get a grip, Eve told herself. She sucked in a deep breath, and leaned close as if sharing a confidence. "I'm already sold. You can ease up now."

His thumb teased over the inside of her wrist. Slowly, he shook his head. "No, I don't think I can."

"Really?" Damn it, she squeaked. Clearing her throat, she said, "Try, okay?"

"How about one taste first?"

"One taste?" Yeah, sounded like a hell of an idea. "You mean..?"

With one small tug, he had her up against him. His free hand flattened on the small of her back, but not in restraint. She in no way felt forced.

She felt . . . seduced.

And wasn't that a unique thing?

"A kiss," he told her, and his breath brushed her lips. "Just a small one."

Would she be able to control herself? Doubtful. Harmony did not have men like him. Her experience was limited. She'd never encountered—

Hot, damp heat touched her lower lip and her thoughts shattered. Lightly, he traced the tip of his tongue to the corner of her mouth and back again, and sure enough, her lips parted.

He didn't overpower her with the kiss. In fact, the contact of his mouth on hers was so light that he somehow lured her into leaning into him, trying to get more.

His head tilted the tiniest bit, his tongue pressed in, touched the edge of her teeth, slicked beyond to meet her tongue . . . And he retreated.

Breathing hard, Eve finally realized that he'd released her. Her eyes fluttered open to find him watching her with so much force, she felt snared.

"Wow."

Something flared in his light brown eyes, an inferno exploding, and she knew she'd just sealed her fate—at least for that night. "So." She tried to gather her thoughts. "How about—"

Someone grabbed her arm from behind. Taken off guard, she stumbled back and almost fell.

The hunk reacted with incredible reflexes. Within a single second, she was free, upright, and somehow behind him.

She heard Roger sneer, "I guess I'm interrupting?"

Oh shit. Double shit. How could she have forgotten about Roger-the-repulsive?

She ducked to the side of her hunk to meet Roger's seething condemnation. A glance at the hunk showed no expression at all. He didn't look angry. Or concerned. He didn't look like a man who'd reacted instinctively to a situation with lightning speed.

"Sorry about that."

"Save your excuses," Roger bit off.

"I wasn't talking to you." She stepped between the men, putting Roger at her back. "I can't imagine how," she said with a smile, "but I forgot that I'm meeting Roger tonight to discuss business."

"Business, huh?"

"He owns this joint. I'm an events coordinator." She lifted her shoulders to share her predicament. "The town doesn't boast a lot of options, so I'm forced here on a regular occasion."

"Forced?" Roger snarled. "Without me, you wouldn't have a business."

Now that was too over the top. Eve prepared to blast him, but he beat her to the punch.

"Find your manners and introduce me."

"Right." She really shouldn't go out of her way to provoke Roger. He was right that without him and his establishments, her business wouldn't be nearly so lucrative. "Roger Sims, proprietor." She gestured toward the hunk. "And you are?"

He smiled.

Propping one shoulder against the wall, the hunk said, "Most people call me Havoc."

"Seriously?" How odd. Sure, he'd caused havoc to her system, but that couldn't be his given name. "Oh, wait. Is that like a fighting label?"

Roger pushed himself closer. "I hope you're joking."

Havoc winked at her.

Read on for
an exciting preview
of
***New York Times* bestselling author**
Carly Phillips's
hot new romance

Cross My Heart

Now available in hardcover

Coming in mass market paperback
July 2007

From HQN Books

The sky was jet black. No stars. No moon. No light to give them away. Tyler Benson led the way to the top of the cliffs with Lilly by his side. Daniel Hunter, their best friend, lagged behind. Lilly held onto Ty's hand. Every once in a while, she'd squeeze tighter, giving away her fear. Otherwise Ty would think this was just another of their adventures. He knew better.

Soon, Ty would start the car, slam it into drive, and then jump out before it toppled off the cliff into the murky quarry waters below. Afterwards, Lilly Dumont would be reported missing. Her uncle's car would be found at the bottom of the lake. Or it wouldn't be found at all. No body would be recovered. Lilly would head for New York, take the new name the three of them had chosen for her, and Ty would never see her again.

All so Lilly wouldn't have to return to her bastard uncle for more abuse. She was only seventeen. She wouldn't survive a month, let alone a year, if she returned to her uncle. The man didn't love *her* but her trust fund, Ty thought.

"Hurry up, Daniel!" Lilly called back to Hunter, breaking the silence. She was probably afraid he'd lose them in the dark.

"It's Hunter," their friend and foster brother muttered loud enough for them to hear.

Ty grinned. Once Ty had told him to go by his last name, the kids at school had stopped calling him "Danny Boy" and Hunter had quit trying to beat the crap out of anyone who got in his face. Hunter and Ty were like real brothers, and Ty looked out for his own. Hunter did the same, which was why Hunter stayed back now, so Ty could have these last few minutes with Lilly.

The locket he'd bought for her burned a hole in his pocket. He'd bought it so she wouldn't forget him. Ever. His stomach cramped, and he halted suddenly.

Lilly bumped into him. "What's wrong? Why are you stopping? We aren't there yet."

Ty swallowed hard. "I just wanted to give you something." He whispered even though nobody was around to hear.

He shoved his hand into his pocket and pulled out the small gold heart. A hot flush washed over him as he held out his hand. Good thing it was dark and she couldn't see his burning cheeks.

"Here," Ty muttered. It wasn't much and that embarrassed him as much as giving the gift.

Lilly accepted the tiny locket. Though it was hard to see, she turned it over in her hand, studying it for so long he shifted uncomfortably on his feet while waiting for her reaction.

"It's beautiful," she finally said, a catch in her voice.

He exhaled his relief. "I . . ." Ty wasn't a guy of many words, and he didn't know what to say now.

"I know." As always, she stepped in, reading and easing his mind. She clasped the heart in one hand and threw her arms around his neck, holding him tight.

Ty couldn't think or even speak past the lump in his throat.

She pulled back suddenly and looked down. She messed with the necklace and somehow she managed to hook the heart around her neck despite the lack of light.

"Thank you," she said softly, meeting his gaze.

He nodded stiffly. "You're welcome."

Seconds of silence passed, neither one of them wanting to say the words but someone had to. They couldn't risk getting caught.

"We need to get moving," Hunter said, joining them. "The longer we spend here, the more we risk getting caught."

Ty nodded. "He's right. We have to go," Ty finally said.

"Okay, then let's do this," Lilly said, and the three friends started forward.

A few minutes later, they walked through the underbrush and came out near the cliff. The car was waiting for them.

"Is it really Uncle Mark's?" Lilly asked, rubbing her hand over the dark blue Lincoln.

Ty nodded. "A buddy of mine knows how to hotwire cars. He owes me a favor for not turning him into the cops, so this was no biggie." Ty had friends in different groups, different places. Pulling this off had been too easy.

"I can't believe we're doing this," Lilly said.

She stared at him, wide-eyed and afraid. But behind the fear, Ty saw her determination. She was strong and gutsy and he was really proud of her.

"It's not like we have a choice," Hunter reminded her.

"I know." She nodded, her dark hair falling over her face before she tucked it behind her ear. "You guys are the best, helping me like this."

"One for all, all for one," Hunter said.

Ty tried not to laugh and embarrass his friend. Hunter always said the dumbest things, but Ty didn't mind. Besides he figured Hunter wasn't thinking any clearer than they were at the moment.

"We're the Three Musketeers," Lilly said, grinning. Just like always, she agreed with her friend to prevent him from being mortified.

Besides she was right. So was Hunter. The three of them were alone in this, and it would bind them forever. Ty stuffed his hands into front jeans pocket.

"So tonight Lillian Dumont dies and Lacey Kinkaid is born." Her voice quivered.

He didn't blame her for being afraid. She was leaving Hawken's Cove, their small upstate New York town. She'd take off for New York City alone with just the summer money the three of them had managed to scrounge up.

"Nobody talks about what happened here tonight. Not ever," Ty reminded them. They couldn't afford for anyone to discover even a part of their plan and piece things together. "Right?" he asked, wanting to hear them say the words. His heart pounded so hard in his chest he thought it would explode.

"Right." Hunter agreed.

"Lilly?" Ty prodded. She had the most to lose if her uncle found out she was alive.

She nodded. "I'll never talk about it." Her gaze remained locked on his, her fingers toying with the little heart around her neck.

Ty stared into her brown eyes and suddenly everything was okay. They'd go back to his mom's house, and he'd sneak into her bedroom so they could hang out and talk all night. They'd be together.

Instead she broke the spell. "I'll never forget what you guys did for me," she said to them both.

She hugged Hunter first and Ty waited, clenching and unclenching his fists.

Then she turned to him and pulled him tight. He held her for the last time, closing his eyes and fighting the fullness in his throat.

"Be careful," he managed to tell her.

She nodded, her hair soft against his cheek. "I'll never forget you, Ty. *Cross my heart*," she whispered, the words for his ears alone.